T
HELL
WITH
POETS

TRANSLATED BY

TO HELL WITH POETS
BAQYTGÚL SARMEKOVA

MIRGUL KALI

TILTED AXIS PRESS

CONTENTS

CONTENTS

THE BLACK COLT

Embarrassed of being deaf in one ear, he worried about missing out on conversations and had a habit of nodding and giggling whenever people as much as twitched their lips, prompting some to wonder if he was soft in the head. The harsh stare of a stranger's eye made him uncomfortable, and he'd fidget and tousle his hair, sprinkled with gray strands that had crept in too early for his age. Especially when a woman came near him, Turar would begin to blink rapidly, get all red and sweaty, then turn white as a sheet, all the while grinning awkwardly and baring his tobacco-stained teeth. Some of the more brazen women in our rural aul had taken note of this and would tease him, pinching his side as they walked by or brushing up against him with their breasts, plump and quivering like intestines filled with sour cream. In those moments, one couldn't help but feel pity for Turar.

It was this Turar that my grandfather had resolved to pluck out of the wicked women's claws by introducing to Zharbagul, his wife's younger sister. He instructed my grandmother to cook the salt-cured meat left over from the winter, mounted his three-wheeled motorcycle, and drove off into town to fetch Zharbagul. Turar grew very thoughtful, and we sensed the stirring of his heart as we watched the ash at the end of his cigarette slowly grow to the length of a finger.

Before long, my grandfather returned with Zharbagul, whose bucket-shaped head bobbed up and down in his sidecar as they rode along the bumpy road. This was the first time we had ever met our aunty whose huge head, dark, rough, trowel-shaped face, and stumpy legs were a strange match with her thin pigtails, wire earrings, and lacy, ruffled dress.

The grin didn't leave Turar's lips until the meal was over. He blinked and nodded to every word. Busy romping around the front yard, we nevertheless kept an eye on the proceedings, and some of us entertained ourselves by watching Turar's every move. At one point in the afternoon, everyone streamed out of the house: my grandfather went to check on the cows, my grandmother hurried to drain the curd, and the women headed home to catch a movie. They dragged along their kids who had been playing with us out in the front yard.

When evening came, Zharbagul got ready to go home. My grandfather kicked the pedal, starting the motorcycle. As they rode away, Zharbagul's twig-like pigtails slapped against her monstrous back. Still grinning, Turar squeezed a cigarette between his yellow-stained teeth and announced, "We're going to have a toi!"

The next day, someone brought over a colt and tied him to a tree in our front yard. It was Turar's gift to my grandfather for helping him find the love of his life, Zharbagul. My grandfather who'd been a cowherd all his life was ecstatic about owning a horse. All of a sudden, he was bustling about brushing the colt's mane and braiding a lucky red string into it, ordering horse tack and sackfuls of oats from town. Cows were all he'd ever known, but now, whenever he got together with the other old men, he chatted about the care and training of horses. He began to sound like someone who owned hundreds of them. "Did you make sure there's enough water?" "Have you checked the hobble?" "See to it that the mice don't chew through the oat bags," he'd insert in the middle of a conversation. "By fall, he'll be old enough to saddle up and take out for a ride," he said and began counting the days. The colt was indeed a beautiful animal, and we couldn't help but stare at him in awe, though he'd whinny when we approached and look askance at us, his nostrils flared, his ears flicking, his forelock flying in the breeze. We named him Qarager.

After Zharbagul visited a few more times, the preparations for the wedding toi began in earnest. My grandmother started beating fleece for new körpe mats for Zharbagul's dowry, and the women scoured local markets for fabric to decorate them with. Turar's family got busy sprucing up their house and repainting the windows and doors.

Then, one wet summer day, while driving his sheep toward the aul, Turar stepped carelessly on the broken end of a downed power line and died, his body burned to a crisp. The adults who had gone to look at his body said, "He was grinning ear to ear when he passed on to the Great Beyond." No one knew if he was beaming at the thought of his beloved Zharbagul or grimacing in pain when the fatal charge struck.

It wasn't in the cards for the thirty-year-old Zharbagul after all to sing the bride's farewell to her family. She came by to pay her respects, whimpering quietly as translucent tears left wet traces on her rough-hewn face.

When the commotion caused by Turar's death quieted down, his brother Sailau showed up in our front yard with a rope in his hand.

"I've come to take the colt, Qabeke!" he said. He must have been preparing for this moment because his voice came out rather loud and firm.

"Which colt?" my grandfather stared at him with the look of a man whose pastures were teeming with herds of horses. His hat tilted back disdainfully along with his head as he looked up at Sailau.

"The colt is ours. I never heard Turar say that he was giving it to you," Sailau said, spitting loudly to the side.

The startled old man stared at the frothy spittle on the ground, then back at Sailau.

"I'm not giving Qarager back," he said bluntly.

"Then I'll see you in court," Sailau shot back.

After that, my grandfather fell into the habit of sighing wearily whenever he stroked Qarager's mane with the red string woven into it. By then, the colt had put on some weight and turned into a shapely, long-limbed horse.

When a court summons came, my grandfather started his motorcycle and rode into town, the brim of his hat bending defiantly backwards in the wind.

No notes or gift deeds had been exchanged between him and the colt's owner Turar, who must have been grinning down upon Qabeke from heaven. Finding himself backed into a corner at the court hearing, my grandfather defended himself: "I spared no expense in raising this colt. I bought feed, I spent time with it, I exerted myself to care for it. He was a foal when I got him, and now he's a yearling colt with a fine mane and tail. I want my expenses paid."

"The colt goes to Sailau, and Qabeke's expenses are to be tallied up and reimbursed," said the judge, bringing the gavel down with a bang.

Back at home, the sullen old man tried to comfort himself by reminding us, "The judge himself said to pay Qabeke's expenses back." Sitting at the dinner table, he drawled the words in a singsong manner, and they did seem to cheer him up.

With the court order in one hand and a rope in the other, Sailau came striding into our front yard again. The front brim of my grandfather's brown hat didn't rise this time. He lowered his eyes and didn't say a word.

Qarager's mane and tail rustled in the wind and his hoofs clattered on the dry, white ground as Sailau led him away. Only when the sound of hoofbeats faded did my grandfather lift his head and murmur, "If we could have taken him to the ambler race next year, he would have won a prize."

Soon enough, Sailau showed up again, holding the same piece of paper in one hand and leading Qarager by the rope with the other. My grandfather's hat tilted up as he stared at him in astonishment. Sailau proceeded to remove four bags of feed from the colt's back and, raising a cloud of dust, dropped them by the door.

"These are for your material expenses, and the rest is here," he said as he handed my grandfather a carefully sealed envelope retrieved from his shirt pocket. Then he walked away with the unburdened Qarager. When the old man's brown hat began convulsing as he abruptly stood up, we thought he'd take off in a sprint after Sailau, lash him with a whip, jump on Qarager, and gallop away across the barren steppe. But we were wrong. He went over to his wife, whose white headscarf blended with the gray smoke from the outdoor cook stove where she was busying herself, pushed her away, and threw Sailau's envelope onto the glowing dung embers. He then walked over to the bags with feed and after gazing at them thoughtfully for a moment, said: "Take them to the cow shed." Then he went into the house.

2018

THE BROWN HOUSE AND THE WHITE ZHIGULI

Roughcast with mud and straw, the brown adobe house never failed to attract swallows. They must have found the house, with its beefy posts, bolt-upright walls, and proud demeanor, tall enough to build their nests on: every spring, they lined the edge of the roof, their fuzzy red-orange necks shimmering in the sunlight.

The inhabitants of the house were equally imposing. Every morning, little old Khabes would throw open its heavy hardwood door and stand out front, the flaps of his brown trench coat pulled back and his hands tucked in his pants' pockets. His black boots were as spotless as his wife's headscarf, and their buttery leather looked even lusher in the sun. Even their dog had an imperious air about him, never growling or sniffing at the hunched mongrels who were always sneaking about the aul in search of food scraps. With his tail pointing straight up, the dog would emerge from his wooden kennel lined with the white goat pelt and stand beside his owner, gazing out in the same direction. You'd never see him disheveled or sulking. He was always alert, always confident.

Sporting thick, carefully brushed hair without so much as a single strand of gray, the seventy-year-old Khabes ambled around his house and, occasionally rumpling and smoothing his low forehead with two long, deep lines, pressed his lean hands against each post and examined the spots where the plaster had fallen off. As soon as he sighted an unsteady post, he'd race in his shiny boots toward the shed where he kept his tools and instruments. He'd emerge dragging along a shovel and an axe and set to work immediately, as if the house was on the verge of collapsing.

"I bought this house from the famous merchant Shughayip for eight oxen. Eight oxen!" he'd exclaim, folding his thumbs down and raising his hands to show the number. "The beams are made of red oak. That's right! Red, not white. They say it took him, the gracious soul, a whole summer and fall to have it hauled a-a-a-all the way from Russia," he said, drawing the sound out as if wishing to reach that faraway land where the wood had come from. If a visitor happened to take an interest in the house, the floodgates would open and Khabes would recount its entire history. Meanwhile, his elderly wife bustled about making tea for the guests, her white headscarf glimmering amid the gray smoke billowing from the samovar.

Next to Khabes's stately home, a handful of nearby saddlebag-style houses, made up of two rooms separated by a narrow corridor, looked rather shabby. Whether intimidated by Khabes himself or by his house, the old men in the neighborhood always deferred to him and were the first to greet him, bowing down and offering both their hands. Even when his dog opened his enormous jaws to give a bark, they neither chased him nor scolded him with the usual "Get lost!"

But one dreary fall awash with nippy, drizzling showers accompanied with whistling, piercing winds, Khabes tripped over his threshold and fell. His compact body went down lightly and neatly, as though he'd been anticipating the fall. His wife's meek, passive eyes grew wide with panic beneath her white headscarf, and she scampered toward the neighboring houses. Dispatches were sent to Khabes's only son and the doctor in the nearby town. The doctor arrived first, his medical bag clattering and clanging with medical tools and glass vials.

Aqsandyq looked suspiciously at her husband's tense, motionless body and tightly-closed eyes, wondering if he was just being obstinate. But the doctor shook his head, prompting a group of neighbors that had gathered round to lower their eyes. Aqsandyq stared in bewilderment. Her eyes filled with tears, and her gaze wandered toward the immaculately clean windows, where the road leading to town was visible. She seemed to be waiting for her son to come and rescue her from this sudden calamity.

It was still raining when he finally arrived, wearing a water-stained leather jacket that was too small for his large body.

"What happened to Khabeke? Is he all right?" he blurted out. Raised by his grandparents and shipped off to a boarding school in town after their death, Yerden always called his father by his nickname.

The doctor took his glasses off and rubbed his eyes as he explained his father's condition.

"He had a stroke. His blood vessels couldn't handle the pressure. The right side of his body, along with his arm and leg, is now paralyzed. Even if he comes to, his speech won't be the same and he may not recognize people. We'll have to wait and see; sometimes people make a full recovery," he said, stretching his eyebrows to look up at the ceiling. He seemed more interested in the massive, closely-spaced red beams than in his patient.

Old Aqsandyq rested her back against the masonry stove, and her eyes brimmed with tears which slowly dripped onto the front of her shiny silk vest.

Khabes' condition didn't improve even after a stay in the town hospital. The doctor was indeed a seer: although Khabes came to his senses, he could no longer speak nor move the right side of his body. It proved difficult for slight, weakly Aqsandyq to tend to her small but stocky husband. Their son stayed at the brown house for a week, puttering about as he pretended to help her. Reluctant to groom his father's thick, jet-black locks, he soon shaved them off. Holding a thimble-sized mirror in his shovel-like hands and sniggering, he tried to show his father the results of his handiwork, but Khabes refused to open his eyes. In the corner by the wood stove, Aqsandyq held her breath, worrying about how the old man who was in the habit of carefully brushing his hair with a fine-tooth comb every day would take to his newly bald head.

Shortly after the son left for town, he returned in a heavy-duty KAMAZ truck that roared and shook the earth as it entered the tiny aul. "You're moving in with me," he announced to his parents and, before they could even respond, playfully picked up a heavy old trunk sitting in the entryway and took it to the truck. Untouched by dust or dirt, the yellow metal panels of the trunk glinted in the sun.

"We didn't expect this, but we're moving. Yerden wants us to go live with him," Aqsandyq hurried to announce their departure, flitting from one neighbor's house to another, her white headscarf gleaming in the twilight. It was difficult to tell whether she was happy, proud, or anxious. The neighbors didn't ask questions and rushed to help, quickly loading Khabes' and Aqsandyq's furniture and belongings into the

KAMAZ. Even old Idayat, who didn't get along with Khabes and annoyed him with his obstinacy, picked up a fire iron leaning against the wall by the entrance and shouted: "Hey, you forgot the poker! Where should I stick the poker? You might end up needing it later!" As he wandered back and forth, not knowing what to do with the iron, his black-gray beard quivered, revealing his distress.

The neighbors helped Khabes, dressed in a gray wool coat and a matching hat, both retrieved from the trunk and smelling of perfume and mothballs, to get from the house to the truck. Idayat's wife Kulyash wrapped a thick blanket around Khabes's legs. None of this impressed Khabes, whose eyes, normally squinty, stared wide in stupor at the dirt road lit up by the truck's headlights. His hat was tilted rakishly back, just like in the old days. He was as well put together as ever.

Aqtös the dog had stayed away from all this commotion. He did not run around or get in the way of anyone, but rather stood by his kennel, ears pricked high and nose in the air. Only when the truck started with a loud noise did he anxiously run toward Aqsandyq, who hurried in her soft little boots toward the truck's cabin. Then he made a strange sound: higher-pitched than a bark, deeper than a whimper, but not quite a howl. As if longing for an answer from Idayat, the whites of whose eyes shone in the twilight as he stood gripping the poker, the dog sniffed the trailing hem of his shapan.

In his leather jacket about to burst at the seams, Yerden clutched the steering wheel, grinning from ear to ear. "You'll live in the regional center now. You'll be big city people! And Khabeke will get back on his feet and be one hell of an old dog," he said patting his father on the shoulder. Taken aback by this show of boldness from her son who had always been wary of his father's temper and enlisted her help if he needed something from him, Aqsandyq first gaped at her son, then glanced timidly at her husband.

Aqsandyq was used to complying with the old man's wishes. She'd never had cash of her own, never gone to the market to buy things for the house. It was Khabes who made all the decisions, took care of everything. He'd made sure they didn't waste or lack for anything. And he made sure to buy his wife a fragrant shampoo every month. When Khabes became debilitated, Aqsandyq, not knowing what to do with the roll of banknotes she kept at the bottom of the trunk, handed it to her son.

On the first day in her son's apartment, Aqsandyq, who'd never been served food before, found it uncomfortable to sit idly across from her daughter-in-law at the table while she poured her tea. But she quickly took to the friendly young woman, whose smile dimpled her tan-colored cheeks and brought mischievous sparkles to her eyes. The daughter-in-law didn't hesitate to tell her that there was no spare space in the apartment, and so their old furniture was left outside. They never remembered the fire poker they'd left at the brown house or, to be exact, in Idayat's hands. The alasha rug Aqsandyq had made over the summer, bending over to wash, dye, spin, then weave the wool, was thrown into the junk shed without so much as being unrolled. The even-tempered, gentle Aqsandyq didn't say a word. Too timid to protest when her son announced that he'd found a buyer for their brown house, she only glanced anxiously at the shriveled, feeble old man who had sunk into the depths of an overly soft mattress. When a pair of deep lines appeared on his forehead, she realized that Khabes had heard his son's announcement. But the old man lay still. Only when his son left the room did he open his eyes and fix his gaze on the chandelier's sparkling crystals. He must have been thinking of the red oak beams in his house.

Eventually, the house was demolished, everything but the timber destroyed. Yerden added the money from the sale to the roll of banknotes in the old trunk and bought himself a white Zhiguli. "Khabeke, the car is a killer! It vrooms!" he told his father after flying all over town in it, his pudgy fingers nearly poking Khabes's face when he tried to demonstrate the car's speed. Nearby, Aqsandyq blinked nervously, startled by her son's brazenness and anxious about her husband's response. But Khabes only knitted his eyebrows, forcing the lines on his forehead to converge, and his body remained stiff as a board.

Their daughter-in-law took to the new car too. She rode around town in it with her husband, bouncing in her seat and revealing her white teeth and dimples as she laughed. They made the rounds collecting körimdik gifts from friends and relatives who wished to see the new car. Later, they invited everyone to their one-bedroom apartment to celebrate their extravagant purchase. When more guests came than they had room for, they pushed Khabes's bed into the corner of the living room. Wary of every twitch in the old man's face, Aqsandyq moved with the bed. Toasts were made, the dombyra was played, songs were sung. Yerden drank a lot of wine. "I saw a strand of gray at your temples, mother," he sang as he staggered over to his mother and planted fervent kisses on her forehead.

But Yerden's excitement over his car, which he'd fire up even for a trip to the grocery around the corner, didn't last long. On a bitterly cold day in late fall, the white Zhiguli skidded on the muddy ice and flipped over, landing on the side of the road. Yerden made it out alive, tumbling out of the car in his jacket, which had bunched up around his back and left his butt exposed. He came home looking like a pig that had been wallowing in the mud and began blubbering uncontrollably as soon as he entered the apartment. It was hard to tell if he was crying over the car, which was damaged beyond repair, or because he felt embarrassed in front of his father. Khabes lay staring at the ceiling. He paid no attention to the high-pitched whimpering, so at odds with his son's bulky frame. Only Aqsandyq knew what her husband might be thinking about: their dog, who had likely grown haggard, not used to eating slops thrown out from people's kitchens, and who'd inevitably be attacked by the hunched, mangy neighborhood dogs; and the swallows who would look for the brown house in the spring and, finding only a pile of debris in its place, hover above it, beating their delicate, trembling wings.

2019

DOGNITY

He lay in the shade, occasionally shaking his head to shoo the flies away from his ears. Rotten flies! Landing on my ears as if their wings would fall off if they didn't! Who knows where else they've been besides Marzhan's unwashed qazan? he thought. Enraged, he snapped his teeth to catch one of the flies, but missed. Someone's shadow fell over him. He looked at the legs, one of which was shorter than the other, and recognized them as belonging to the lame Eltai. A few nights ago, he had seen a man peeping into the windows in the front yard and, taking him for a thief, charged at him and bit him with all his might. When he realized that the person had been Eltai and that he had bitten his shorter leg, he immediately regretted hurting him. Marzhan didn't pat him on the head, either.

His bowl, which hadn't seen any slops poured into it for two days, had dried up in the sun. He wagged his tail and licked the dusty hem of Eltai's pants, trying to redeem himself before him. He even tried to smile a little.

Humans are lucky. They can smile and laugh if they want... he thought to himself.

"Aqtös, Aqtös! Such a smart dog! You just don't recognize your neighbors at night, but otherwise you're a good dog, aren't you?" When Eltai said this, he felt a rush of affection for him. He pinned his ears back and looked up at him with wide eyes, as if pleading with Eltai to be forgiven for having been so reckless and biting someone so kind. When the man threw two pieces of bread to him, Aqtös was beside himself. Wishing to thank Eltai, he lifted his paw and brushed it against the man's palm, smearing mud all over it. Then, anticipating a punishment for his blunder, he brought his muzzle toward the man's kirza boots. Instead of kicking him, Eltai stroked him behind his ear. The dog had been craving human touch for a while now, and the gesture nearly moved him to tears. No one had petted him since the death of his owner Talap.

Aqtös had been upset at Talap for leaving him in the stingy Marzhan's care. "He had a weak heart," "It was that damned alcohol that finished him," "He was a good man," said the people who had come to Talap's wake. Aqtös planted himself by the door that day and lay quietly as if waiting for them to comfort him too. When Talap's six-year-old son rushed behind the men who came out of the house carrying his father's body, the dog ran after the boy. The body was placed in a vehicle, which raised a thick cloud of dust as it drove away toward the cemetery. The adults picked up the crying boy, all covered in dust, and took him back into the house. Wishing to pay his last respects to the owner, the dog decided to follow the vehicle to the cemetery six kilometers away. When he finally reached the cemetery, his burning lungs in pain, he saw the men bury Talap and realized he would never see him again. Long after the pallbearers and mourners left, he roamed around the grave, sniffing the freshly excavated soil. He searched for the familiar sour smell of alcohol mixed with sweat but found only a peculiar scent of dredged-up soil, fragrant from the broken blades and roots of young grass. Was it the scent of a fresh grave or of a life that hadn't quite submitted to death yet?

He snapped up a piece of bread lying in front of him and gulped it down. It is said that a dog remains where it's fed. Although a couple of pieces of bread weren't enough to fill him up, he was grateful to Eltai for his kindness and forgiveness. He wanted him to stick around and maybe even tell a story or two. On the days his late owner came home drunk and received a tongue-lashing from Marzhan, he would come sit with the dog, caressing him and telling him of his woes. "Look at these two shoddy dogs cozying up to each other," Marzhan would say in disgust. "This dog is better than all of you," Talap replied, and Aqtös would get all puffed up.

But Eltai didn't linger. His hip jerked up and down as he limped away. Aqtös decided that tomorrow, instead of lying around and waiting in vain for food, he would help Eltai drive his sheep home. He returned to his spot in the shade and was about to plop down and get back to entertaining the flies when suddenly his stomach gave a violent heave. His insides began to burn, and the taste of blood came to his tongue. His throat turned dry, and he stuck his tongue out as he staggered frantically about. He had no idea what was happening. They must have shot me like Kendebai's bitch who wouldn't stop whelping, he thought. He felt too weak to look around and see who shot him. Gasping for air and yearning desperately for water, he staggered toward the door and scratched against it. But he had little hope that Marzhan, who had turned a blind eye when her drunk of a husband was dying from alcohol poisoning, would give him so much as a drop of water. He decided to find his friend Eltai. He gathered all his strength and slowly dragged himself toward his house. Eltai won't let me die; when he sees me like this, he will do everything he can to save me. As he made his way toward the door, he saw Eltai pull up the blinds and glance at him. He waited for the familiar clank of the hook-and-eye latch. His strength was failing him; he could barely stand, let alone move. He felt like weeping at his helplessness. Humans are lucky; they can cry their eyes out if they want to, he thought.

Many years ago, Talap had brought him home in an empty vodka box. "I traded this puppy for a bottle of imported booze!" Talap had boasted. Later, in the aul dog fights where the main prize was alcohol, Aqtös did his best to make Talap proud of him. Once, he'd had part of his ear ripped off and his leg muscle torn up by one of his more vicious opponents. Another time, he had had a gory fight with an Alabai dog. In the end, he lost, and Talap had to buy the winner's owner a bottle of vodka. Overcome with guilt, he suffered his injury in silence, even when the pus began to ooze from his wound and attract flies.

He tried to lift his head to see if the door opened, but a fog descended over his eyes, and he retched so violently it felt as though his stomach were turning inside out. He wanted to cry but was only able to give a weak, whimpering howl. Humans are lucky; they can cry as much as they want to... After that, he felt nothing.

Late that night, Eltai dragged the dead dog's body toward the ash-covered trash heap outside the aul. He dug a shallow hole, threw the dog's corpse along with the poison he had earlier added to the bread in it, and covered it with several shovelfuls of soil. At home, he took a cold shower to stop sweating, put on an ironed calico shirt, and headed to Marzhan's house, which still had its lights on at this late hour. He quickened his pace as he thought of cupping Marzhan's breasts spilling out of her silk robe, when his short leg suddenly tripped and he nearly fell. The dog bowl lay at his feet. What was the bowl to him when he had just got rid of the dog—the last reminder of Talap's existence? He kicked it awkwardly with his short leg. Then he came to the door and whispered, "Marzhan honey, sweet Marzhan, I'm here!" The weathered door, whose old hinges had never seen grease, creaked as the hostess threw it wide open.

2017

MONICA

The chin of the taxi driver, a young man in cheap plastic sunglasses, jerked rhythmically up and down as he masticated his gum. Occasionally, he blew a bubble, and when it popped, his saliva spattered everywhere, some of it landing on my face. I sat in the front passenger seat looking at the sprawling yellow steppe behind the window, but out of the corner of my eye, I could feel him sneaking cautious glances at my face and skirt, which was two inches too short to shield my bare knees.

Soon, the yellowish, moss-grown roofs tucked between drab-colored hills overgrown with squat tamarisk bushes came into view. The squalid aul looked like a sloppy woman's kitchen. The graveyard, which used to be nestled at the base of the hills, now sprawled out to the edge of the main road. A march of corpses, I thought to myself. I told the driver to stop and got out of the car. It took me a while to find the grave of my brother, who had once taken up residence at the very edge of this village of the dead. The grave was now in the middle of the cemetery; its weather-beaten headstone was crumbled, and the engraving, bleached by the sun, was barely legible. My memory of him had also begun to fade: I didn't sigh as much as I used to. There were no tears either; I didn't even feel sad.

When I got back in the car, the music blasting on the stereo threatened to shatter the flimsy metal exterior of the vehicle. I felt like snapping at the obnoxious driver but was overcome by a bout of listlessness.

"Are you Bolat-agha's daughter?"

"Mhm."

"I saw him drunk in front of the corner store the other day. He said he had a headache, so I gave him some money."

"Mhm."

"I heard you you're a big boss at some place in the city..."

"Mhm."

Looking satisfied with his "small talk," he adjusted his flimsy sunglasses and squared his shoulders. Then he straightened the collar of his soiled shirt and looked down at me over the top of his glasses.

By evening, the news of my arrival reached our neighbors and relatives, and they began gathering at our house. After showering me with greetings and questions, they sat staring at me as if they were about to eat me alive. I could sense them relishing the thought of sharing a juicy bit of gossip with their friends later on. After tea, I stepped outside for a breath of air and found one of my sisters-in-law, tasked with preparing dinner at the wood stove out in the front yard, in the entry room, trying on one of my shoes. The other shoe lay by the door with its heel pointing upward. Trying not to embarrass her, I joked, "If you take good care of my brother, I'll buy you a pair of shoes just like these for your birthday." The brown freckles on her face darkened as she lowered her eyes.

In the distance, I saw Monica running towards our house, the hem of her thick, hand-knit sweater dress, thrown on despite the warm spring day, flapping around her legs. Nobody in the village remembered this simple-minded older woman's real name—Monshaq; even the children called her Monica. I could never figure out if they did so out of pity or because they were mocking her by likening her dull face, with its slit eyes and snub nose, to Monica Belucci's. She thrust herself at me, wrapping her arms around my shoulders and murmuring something hastily into my ear. I felt hot tears trickling down my neck.

"Why are you crying, silly? Now, now, calm down," I said, stroking her hair, but she didn't stop. She kissed me, drooling all over my face. Soon, there wasn't a dry spot left on it. She must have drunk ayran or nibbled on a piece of qūrt right before she came, for the scent of sour milk hit my nostrils every time her mouth touched my face. Her heavy metal earrings swayed and shook as she sobbed. I used to know her language, but I'd completely forgotten it by now.

My mother told me that she shared a room with Monica at the maternity ward when she was giving birth to me. She said she couldn't forget the image of Monica cradling her big, chubby baby in her arms and marveling at her as if she were a doll. But her family decided that Monica wasn't fit to take care of her newborn and, without telling her, gave the baby away to some childless couple. "When Monica learned she had lost her child, she bawled in despair. Her breasts became swollen with milk, and she was in a lot of pain, poor wretch," my mother recalled. I learned that Monica would later come and sit staring at me, bundled up in the cradle, for hours.

Hopping and skipping, I grew up with Monica around. She lived with relatives on her father's side, who kept her busy with chores like carrying water, tending to sheep, and pulling weeds. But whenever she had a free minute, she would always come to play with us. I became used to her sneaking up behind me to squeeze me in a hug in the midst of play or taking on my enemies when I got into fights. It was that same Monica who was now crying on my shoulder. After wiping her face with her sleeve, she lifted the hem of her dress to show me an ugly scar on her stomach. "Don't, it's not okay to do this," I said, pulling the hem down. From her babbling, I made out that she had recently had surgery to remove her appendix.

She was by my side all three days that I was in the aul. She would show up early in the morning at our house, greeting me with her toothless, sunken grin that looked more like a scowl, and stayed there until evening.

God knows what had gotten into me, but one day I asked her who the father of her child was. As if that wasn't enough, I made a motion with my arms as if I were cradling a baby. The question startled her. She stared at me with a look of horror in her face, then, sending the hem of her sweater dress flying, bolted toward the door. She made a racket in the entry room, kicking aside the pitchers and wash-basins on her way out. In the evening, when I saw Monica with her badly-cut, disheveled hair peeping in from behind the entrance door, I got up and went outside. She looked nervously over her shoulder and pressed something into my hand. It was an old photograph of three men in military uniforms. I peered into the yellowish, fading picture with creased corners and recognized the face of a handsome young fellow with a moustache, standing between two Russian men. Yes, it was him. The old Sarja's eldest son who lived in Almaty. I had seen him when he had come to the aul to attend a couple wedding tois. I remembered the reverence with which the aul residents had spoken of him. "Turns out, his wife is a theatre actress."

"They say his sons study abroad." "He's going to take Sarja to a fancy foreign resort next year." "He's a university professor himself." "He'd even gifted that crazy Monica a pair of earrings…" It was as though they were telling fables to each other.

The old Sarja didn't want to send her youngest sister Monica to an asylum, so when their parents died, she took her in to live with her.

Monica pointed at the man with a moustache and said, "Babba." Then she widened her eyes, threw another glance over her shoulder, brought her finger to her lips, and said, "Shh." I felt somehow that I had always known this secret of hers. I wasn't at all surprised. Or maybe I'd lost my ability to feel anything.

I left before dawn the next day. Monica must have been heartbroken when she rushed over to our house in the morning with her tongue hanging out like a giddy dog—only to find that I was gone.

2017

MÖLDIR

There are times when I feel remorse before my characters.
For they, too, have hearts, and their hearts can ache...

My former classmates decided to have a reunion for the tenth anniversary of our high school graduation. After we had recounted all the news we could think of, the subject of Möldir inevitably came up.

"She lives out there in the steppe, herding sheep. She has five hundred sheep, a child, and a husband. Her sheep bear twins, so she's been the leading shepherd in the area," said one of the guys who liked to crack jokes. "Which Moldir?" I said, batting my fake eyelashes. I wanted to make sure they knew how removed I'd been from shabby aul life since I moved to the city. I knew that having such short memory would greatly improve my reputation among them.

But of course, I knew Möldir. She was a sheep herder's daughter. When their family had moved into our aul, they had nowhere to live, so, in exchange for a sheep, they rented an old shack in our backyard. Before long, a dark-skinned girl came running up to our house to say hello to my mother. Her tightly coiled curls bounced whenever she moved her head. Her name was Möldir, a word that aptly described those stunning, luminous eyes whose near-translucence must have struck her parents when she was born. Her long, curly eyelashes were even prettier than my doll's. I felt jealous as I looked at her out of the corner of my squinty eyes. I decided to ignore her or else treat her as inferior; after all, she lived in a shack that belonged to us.

"Looks like you're the same age as my daughter. You can be playmates," said my mom. She had barely finished speaking when I interrupted her. "Do you know the multiplication table? How much is nine times five?" I rattled off, turning toward Möldir. Her curls quivered as she shook her head. "I don't play with ignorant people," I said and, opening one of the thick volumes lying next to me, began reading aloud from it. I wanted to show her that I was better than her. She looked at me with curiosity.

She turned out to be industrious. She woke up early and got herself busy with chores: fetching water from the pump, beating carpets, and even helping to pull weeds in our vegetable garden. In the meantime, I'd lay in the shade reading.

In September, she joined the class I was in. I watched the drops of sweat break out on her nose as she timidly sang in the music class. She had an amazing voice, and everyone held their breath, listening to her. The teacher, an impressionable man, had tears in his eyes as he patted her on the head. But she lived in our shack, which meant that she was my underling, and underlings must not outshine their superiors.

"Excuse me, teacher, but she has lice in her hair. I saw it yesterday," my voice rang out in the silent classroom. The next day, I found Möldir's mom sitting on a wooden saki platform outside the shack and squashing lice in her daughter's hair.

After that, Möldir became my puppet. I delegated to her simple chores like sweeping the front yard and locking up the calves in a pen. Her curls bounced as she rushed about, cheerfully following my orders. If I saw her playing with other girls in the class, I didn't speak to her for a couple of days.

Over time, Möldir's parents built themselves a house and, after throwing a housewarming party, moved out from our shack. I was disappointed and worried that she wouldn't listen to me anymore. One evening, I was driving the calves towards our house when I saw Möldir waiting for me by the gate. She opened the door to the cow pen and helped me remove the calves' hobbles.

"I'll be singing at a concert tomorrow," she said. "No, you won't," I replied, glaring at her. The next day, I caught sight of Möldir skipping by our house in white sandals, her pretty, hairspray-coated braids shimmering in the sunlight, and decided not to go to the concert.

When the summer break began, Möldir's family left for a summer pasture to let their livestock graze on abundant grass in the steppe. She didn't return to school in September. Before long, I overheard a neighbor telling my mom, "I saw Toiqozha's wife with her daughter at the women's clinic. I asked her what was going on, but she didn't say much. So I found out from nurses that her daughter had been raped by a hired shepherd and that she's pregnant now. They were there for an abortion." My mom glanced at me, her eyes widened with alarm, but I pretended to keep reading my book. The letters jumped and scattered before my eyes while all kinds of thoughts raced through my mind. I was cunning enough to secretly finish two volumes of *The Thousand and One Nights*, so I had some idea of the intimate relations between men and women and of childbirth. Möldir's misfortune made me feel at once glad and terrified. I was quick to spread the news among my classmates, who had unexpectedly matured over the summer, losing their disheveled hair and snotty faces. The girls were frightened and the boys grinned mysteriously at each other.

Möldir showed up in the beginning of the second quarter. Her tight curls had somehow unfurled, turning into lusterless waves, and her eyes were cloudy, like a mirror that hadn't been wiped for a long time. Already tired of the whispers trailing in her wake and the many eyes following her every move, she was now stalked by random men, who often loitered by her house at night. The music teacher too bothered her for a while, promising to take her to the regional singing contests if she took private lessons with him. The following year Möldir dropped out of school.

"Oh, you're talking about Möldir who dropped out of school in ninth grade?" I said, returning to my classmates' conversation. Perhaps, right this moment, she stood gazing toward the horizon as she waited for the sheep to arrive from pasture, her hand propped against her forehead to shade those striking, luminous eyes from the bright red glow of the setting sun.

2018

THE NIGHT THE ROSE WEPT

He finally made a visit. Though I'd always known he'd show up, I couldn't help but worry that it was one of those wishes that would come true but not in the way you'd expect. He rang the bell twice. I sensed him going through the delightful turmoil of hopeful anticipation mixed with doubt and hesitation. All of it based on the sound of the bell. I had run through the scene in my head a million times—me answering the door, him greeting me—but there would always be a stray detail that left me unsatisfied, forcing me to adjust the scene in my mind again and again. And now, the imagined scene was about to become reality.

I opened the door. He came in.

"I hope I'm not bothering you by coming here," he said. He must have been nervous, since he even forgot to say hello.

"Well, actually, I was just about to go to bed…" I mumbled. This obviously wasn't true; I'd been waiting a whole week for this visit.

"I'm sorry. I should've called you in advance."

He handed me a shiny plastic bag with some sweets in it, then began undoing the laces on his shoes. I immediately regretted my silly posturing, "Well, welcome to my house then!" He flashed a bright smile and headed toward the living room. The hall was narrow, and he brushed against me as I stood with my back to the wall to let him pass. I felt a flicker of desire kindle deep within me as I caught a whiff of nice cologne mixed with the scent of alcohol. He had certainly had some wine to work up his courage. I wanted to know what he felt when his shoulder grazed my breast covered in a light silk fabric.

"I was out with friends and I completely forgot what time it was," he said with an apologetic smile. He sat down in the living room but didn't look around as though this were an everyday occurrence. He took no notice of the wallpaper I'd put up a couple of days ago and the rug I'd recently bought. I'd even bought some plants, though I'd never had the patience to take care of them. A strange mixture of anxiety and desire came over me. Perhaps I shouldn't have bothered to redecorate the apartment after all. I chuckled to myself as I glanced at the rose I'd bought to make the living room look more appealing. I'd replanted it in an earthenware pot, even though roses don't grow indoors.

We sat in silence for some time. He smiled, gazing at me. "You're beautiful even when you're about to go to bed," he said. A surge of heat ran through my body. Why was I so eager to seem indifferent, pretending I was going to sleep? Why had I put on pink lipstick if I was going to bed? He knew I was waiting for him tonight, that I was eager to be with him. He cautiously embraced me and gently drew me toward him. Though, perhaps, "drew me toward him" might be a bit of an exaggeration; in reality, he might not have done much of anything or he might have simply placed his hand on my arm. It was I who leaned closer to him and laid my head on his shoulder. When I felt the fresh, carefully ironed fabric of his shirt against my skin, I remembered his wife—a light-skinned, slightly plump lady I'd met at a wedding toi last year. She must be an exemplary wife.

"If a woman is not married by her thirties, she's got something on her mind. Single women are a danger to society," she told me.

"For a society or for those women who watch over their husbands like peewits watch over their nest?" I retorted.

"They are no danger to the women who watch over their husbands. Not a single man will trade a spouse who fills his house with joy for someone who thinks only of herself and who has her horns locked with time as she struggles in vain to stop her aging. But they are a danger to society. They neither contribute to improving demographics nor help bring comfort into men's lives, so their lives are meaningless," she said with assurance. Then, as if to signal the end of our conversation, she cast a haughty glance around the room. The bright miniature beads on her golden necklace caught the light from the restaurant chandeliers and shimmered, as if to declare her victory.

"You're quite self-assured," was all I said. It was silly to get agitated and argue with her. I looked at her husband, sitting by her side. A tall, darker-skinned man. Though he clearly had heard our conversation, he made sure to stay away from it and pretended to seek advice on some car parts from nearby men. Annoyed by the woman's words, I began entertaining a rather wicked idea. How did I miss him? His large forehead suggested generosity, his brown eyes, which lit up when he smiled, kindness, and his relaxed face, thick brows, and angular nose were attractive in a way that felt truly masculine. My staring at him made his wife suspicious, and, reluctant to start a quarrel, I looked away. I'd already formed my opinion of him. And though this took only seconds, his watchful wife too realized what had happened. As I eyed her husband, she scrutinized me.

Soon, a singer began her performance. At the first sounds of lively music, a man sitting at our table grabbed the self-assured woman by her chubby arms and whisked her away to the dance floor. It was the time to act.

"We won't get into trouble if we go for a twirl, will we?" I said smiling. Surprised by my remark, he laughed awkwardly, then nodded. I felt the warm touch of his hands through the thin nylon fabric of my dress. I was reminded of a hot-water bottle which my grandmother used to put on my back, feet, and belly when I'd catch cold as a kid and which made me feel tranquil. He was so close to me that he too seemed to take notice of my nervous breathing. I saw that he was enjoying our closeness. As we danced, he asked about my work and my situation. When he learned I was a writer, he became even more intrigued. He asked what I wrote about, and when I told him that I was thinking of exploring unexpected subjects and novel ideas, that I wanted to open up conversations on less-talked-about, forbidden themes, he realized a four-minute dance may not be enough. I knew his interest was piqued and that he wanted to hear more. He said he'd drop in at my workplace when he'd get a chance. All the while, I sensed another pair of eyes peering at me from the other end of the room. Pangs of jealousy and, soon enough, exasperation were rousing in their owner. I knew it wasn't wise to stay any longer, so after saying goodbye to the hosts, I left.

I had forgotten how it all started. I lay my head on his shoulder and gently stroked the collar of his shirt with the tips of my fingers. This shirt that his wife so carefully washed and ironed was mine now! This was surely my ultimate weakness:

the meanest thoughts would occur to me during the most emotional or important moments. Even when I wept with happiness, I'd find a moment to take a close, unsparing look at the women standing by my side as they shared in my joy. I might notice a lipstick smudge on my friend's teeth as she laughed with abandon, and a cynical thought would cross my mind. Or I might spot my other friend, standing apart from everybody and barely smiling because she was self-conscious of the wrinkles that appeared on her face when she laughed too hard. But there was no time to waste on random thoughts. I closed my eyes, feeling as though I'd finally grasped the happiness I'd sought for so long. When he brushed my hair away from my face, the wedding ring on his finger glinted, reflecting the overhead light. It was as if the ring was mocking me, saying, "It's just temporary, get yourself together." But I only clung closer to him, reluctant to give up this precious moment of joy.

"Why did you want me to come?"

"I like you and I think you like me too."

He kissed me on the forehead. The only sound that interrupted the languid silence was the incessant beat of my heart. A century seemed to have passed since he kissed my forehead, and I waited impatiently for a kiss on the lips. The gentle touch of his hands on my shoulder blades burned my skin, but I thought to myself: even if I burnt to ashes, I would never let him go. The faint smell of alcohol on his breath was making me drowsy. I tried to fix in my mind his every gesture, every glance, even the movements of his pupils. When he embraced me, pulling me closer to himself, I wanted to feel his entire body against my body. I began to unfasten the buttons on his shirt, and when a couple of them got stuck in the tight buttonholes, I inwardly cursed them. It was as if the buttons put up a fight on behalf of his wife. When he began to unzip my dress, I reached up to switch off the lamp. The light in the hall cast only a dim light in the room. His lips grazed my neck and shoulders, entrancing my mind and hypnotizing my body. The woman holding him tight in her arms, showering his chest with fiery kisses, pushing away the dress he had taken off, pulling off his shirt wasn't me. It seemed like someone else. I wavered between dream and reality, and it felt both sweet and strange. I realized that if I slipped out of his embrace, this fairytale feeling would disappear. Just like Cinderella, I'd be back in this gray, grim reality, left with nothing.

Soon he got ready to leave. He put his shirt back on, carefully fastening every button. Looking at my drawn face, he took me in his arms again and comforted me. "We'll meet again." I nodded. But I wasn't certain if our future meetings would excite me in the same way, bring me the same emotions.

"Well, I'm off."

After he left, I lay my head on the pillow, wishing to preserve every moment of that sweet euphoria, which seemed to have passed in the blink of an eye, and yearning to float again among those treasured memories.

In the morning, I discovered that the potted rose had turned pale. When I gently stroked its petals, a single drop of water rolled down its stem. Meant to grow in the natural soil of the fields and gardens, it would never get used to living in a pot. In that moment, I felt sad—not for the weeping rose but for myself.

2015

THE TAMING OF AQTORY

The sound of the doorbell woke me up. I went to the door and pressed my ear against it. I immediately recognized my landlord by her habit of sniffing repeatedly while scrunching up her nose. I took a minute to think about what I was going to say to her, but nothing worthwhile came to mind. Lying becomes natural when you have no choice. I used to feel ashamed whenever I had to tell lies, blushing and sniffling, terrified that I'd be caught. But I didn't care anymore. Nowadays, if someone were to tell me they were tired of my lies, I would try even harder to convince them. And even if I didn't, even if my falsehoods made no sense, without batting an eye, I would still stand by my lie without moving a single muscle in my face.

"Open the door! How long do you think you'll last cooped up inside?" The raspy voice was followed by an obnoxious snort that reversed the flow of fluids slowly moving down her nostrils. A round lady in her early sixties, she had seemed nice enough early on—that is, back when I used to regularly pay my rent. Her full body radiated generosity, and her smooth, oily face always seemed to be smiling. Even her habit of constantly sniffing, which made her appear childlike, created an impression of sincerity. But in the four months since I lost my job, the number of people and things that irritated me had multiplied, and one of those people was my landlord.

I opened the door.

"I'll pay tomorrow."

"Honey, just clear it out now. That's all I want."

"Give me till tomorrow."

"Don't make me laugh, ainalaayn."

When I was little, my grandmother would stroke my head and say "ainalaayn," a word that sounded so warm and kind. I later learned that "ainalaayn" might have been an ancient chant of a shaman willing to sacrifice himself by taking on another's illness. But the meaning of words seems to change over time, and now, I couldn't think of a single word that sounded meaner than this woman's "ainalaayn."

"Tomorrow."

"Tomorrow? What, you're going to win the lottery tomorrow?"

"Probably not."

I tried to smile but instead produced a grimace that made me look like I was about to cry. I looked at her with the pitiful eyes of someone hoping for yet another act of mercy. Since I was a child, I'd had the habit of imagining my every movement as though it were reflected in a mirror. But at this moment, even I didn't feel sorry for myself. I was repulsed. The landlord, too, seemed to feel disgust rather than pity.

"I'll be back with the police tomorrow!" she said, giving another snort that sent some unsightly fluids back into her nasal cavity as she turned to leave. By then, her nasal voice began sounding rather pleasant to me.

I felt bitter about my helplessness and ineptitude. I had no other skills or talents besides writing. I had looked for jobs, and learned I wasn't even good enough to be a janitor. I hadn't had anything to eat since yesterday morning. My cellphone had been silent for a while; only the bank called occasionally to inform me that they were raising the interest rate on my loans. I had to come up with money. But how? There was nothing left to sell in the apartment. The latest sacrifice was my computer, where many of my stories and musings were stored. The writings I used to hoard like priceless treasures suddenly lost all meaning; I even forgot to copy them before I sold the computer. All I wanted was to find a way out of my miserable situation. Perhaps it's true what they say: that people turn into animals when they are hungry.

Still, I didn't have anything worth selling. The only riches I'd accumulated by my mid-thirties were several shelves stuffed with books, whose characters had infected me with their helplessness and grief. I decided to sell the books. I even calculated how much I'd get from some rare volumes I'd hunted down in the remotest corners of the country: it might be enough to cover the missed rent and one month of expenses.

I filled two large checkered bags with books and dragged them to the central market. After setting up my wares, I began asking the passersby if they'd be interested in books. "Books?" they asked, caught off-guard, and inquired how much they cost. When I told them what I thought was a fair price for my treasures, they laughed and shook their heads. A laugh can be kind, scornful, joyous, mocking, hopeful, helpless... The way these people chuckled was reluctant and uncomfortable as though I were a feeble-minded woman whose antics they found inappropriate to laugh at. Yes, that was it. They thought I was out of my mind. I was out of my mind thinking that my books were worth something and that I'd make money by selling them. Those in their right mind don't need books. I ended up exchanging my books for a couple of days' worth of food, with a man who wore fogged-up glasses. I didn't regret it. In fact, I was rather glad not to have to lug the heavy bags back home.

My phone rang. I figured it was the bank calling and ignored it, but a moment later, a message arrived. "Where are you? Drop me a line?" The man who texted me had once told me that he liked me. I had had a suspicion where it might lead and told him in no uncertain terms what I thought of him. Otherwise, what other hopes would a man who reached the age of the Prophet entertain? I began to avoid him. This was my understanding of dignity; his, however, was different. His dignity was hurt; he couldn't stand hearing such unpleasant words from some siskin like me. The feeling that arose in him was closer to revenge than dignity. In a matter of weeks, I was ousted from the literary circles and lost my job and friends. Though in the beginning people who I had thought of as friends supported me, with time, they too had distanced themselves from me. In any case, their sympathy didn't bring food to my table.

I thought about all this for a while. No one cheered or patted me on the back for standing up for myself. Early on, I had felt I had done what was right, but no one seemed to care. And though I was now ready to knock on the door and ask for a job, I still pleaded with God to make my path easier. But my prayer—of a bishara incapable of anything but writing—must have been lost in transit because it never reached God.

I picked up the phone when he called. His voice was slightly hoarse. "You disappeared," he said. The stress from all the ordeals of the last few months had suddenly caught up to me, and I began sobbing. He took my crying as an apology.

"All right, no need to cry. Are you done being naughty?" he comforted me. I imagined him grinning and saying to himself, "Looks like she's settled like qymyz in a leather skin."

The poverty and hunger will bend and break even a proud giant. Six months ago, I saw things very differently, and the person who I was back then now felt like a stranger. The world was lily-white, and people were full of goodness. And now? Those smiling eyes, friendly faces—all seemed fake.

Feeling as if I had finally figured how to get out of my trap, I began to get dressed. My sense of dignity was long gone: it had burst into flames and burned away like dry reeds, leaving nothing behind, not even ashes.

When I showed up at the designated place, he opened the door himself. He was wearing a track suit that looked too tight on him. I wasn't sure if he put it on because he found it comfortable or simply to look younger. This time though, I was determined to keep my thoughts to myself. No one was perfect; even a man known to the entire country for his magnanimity and wisdom was bound to have disagreeable traits. He squeezed me in his arms. His cologne, which smelled like my younger brother's, must have made him feel attractive, but inside, I was suffocating.

"People told me you've been selling books at the market."

I wished he didn't say this. But I didn't get angry. Instead, I smiled to let him know that I'd put up with anything.

"You've changed so much."

I'd once seen a wild horse, born to roam the steppes, leap toward the sky as she was being tamed. It was painful to watch Aqtory scream and widen her eyes when the bit was pulled and the bloody foam sprayed from her mouth. Drenched in sweat, she bucked and kicked for a long time but eventually gave in.

In the end, there was no meeker horse in our aul than Aqtory. The spirited animal that no one could get close to had come to be ridden by every boy in the neighborhood.

All my troubles were nothing compared to what I was yet to experience. When he wrapped his slim arms around my waist, I didn't know what to do. If I slipped out of his grip, I'd go back to my meager life. I thought of my landlord who would show up at my door tomorrow with policemen to evict me. I closed my eyes and thought of a musician I met a year ago. A very talented man who spoke as though he was singing. Our affair was brief and platonic, but I was filled with regret when he had left.

It had been a while since I'd thought of the musician. When his image appeared in my mind, the longing that had been buried deep in my heart resurfaced, along with the memory of many regretful, sleepless nights. The old arms wrapping themselves around my waist turned into the musician's strong arms. The purplish lips hiding artificial teeth became fiery and magical, lips that seemed to sing when they parted. I was afraid to open my eyes and lose the fragile vision. But I did eventually. The head that lay next to mine on the bed was gray. That was the reality.

I had paid off my debts and returned to my old workplace. The long, gray days transformed into bright, fun-filled ones. My friends began seeking my company again, and I chose not to remind them of the past. I welcomed them with a smile and kept my disillusions to myself. In fact, I didn't even feel upset. It all turned out just as I expected.

The landlord who once pounded on my door as if we were being raided by a warring tribe now showered me with uncommon kindness. Every evening she came by, sniffling and wheezing, with a pot of hot sorpa. "It's cold today, drink up," she'd say refusing to take no for an answer. All resentments and disagreements between us had vanished.

One day, as I was returning home from work, I spotted a sparrow who was pecking at some bread crumbs scattered around for the pigeons. She didn't notice the cat who was sitting at a distance, watching her. When the cat began to crawl slowly toward her, keeping its body close to the ground, the bird sensed danger and flew off. She quickly returned, however, and picked up a stray crumb. Then she walked a safe distance away and stood there for a while. Coming back for another crumb was too risky. Yet flying away was simply unthinkable; how could she give up such an abundance of food? I might just have a taste of one more crumb, she must have decided in the end. She alighted a little closer and had just begun pecking when the hungry-eyed cat pounced, sinking its claws into her body. I could have thrown a rock at the cat and tried to rescue the sparrow. But I wanted to witness the demise of the sparrow. Squeezing the trembling bird in its mouth, the cat looked around cautiously and darted toward the back of the apartment building.

In the morning on the way to work, I turned toward the rear of the building. The snow was dotted with blood, and there were feathers scattered all over the place.

2015

ARMANGUL

Chasing her dreams, Armangul arrived in Astana. Well, let's not get all warm and mushy just because her name means Dream Flower. Her main goal was to find a decent job and marry a suitable young man if he happened to cross her path. It's not that the men in her aul were deficient. It was just that none of the six single men back home had begun considering marriage. By the time they came to their senses, Armangul would have wilted, figuratively speaking. She handed the taxi driver a scrap of paper on which her mother had written the address of her böle, a maternal cousin. On the drive from the train station, she marveled at the magnificent city sights, her mouth agape, and her throat eventually became so dry that she began feeling thirsty. "It would be great if böleshka had tea ready," she mused.

She had to buzz the bell six times before she detected any signs of life in the apartment. Finally, the door swung open, and there was her cousin with only her underwear on. She yawned and said, "I was having a dream of Botik calling me. Silly me, I thought it'd be fine not to pick up the phone, but it's only you," and headed towards a room at the back of the apartment. Her cousin didn't invite her in, but she didn't slam the door in her face either, so Armangul followed her. She had imagined that her böle would get the tea piping hot, all the while showering her with emphatic questions and becoming emotional as she reminisced of home. But böle just plopped onto a wrinkled bed, disappearing in its folds. Armangul remained standing in the middle of the room, feeling uncertain. Just as she was about to put down her bag, she tripped over a pair of high heeled shoes, causing them to teeter and then fall over.

"Ugh! Just take your jacket off and lie down next to me. I need to get some sleep before we talk," her böle said. Armangul looked at the bed where her cousin lay sprawled, leaving no room for her, and decided to sit instead.

Armangul wasn't sure how much time had passed before her cousin began waking up. She stretched and yawned. Then she reached for her phone and began scrolling down its screen, smiling and murmuring to herself. "Idiot!" she then said in a singsong voice. Suddenly she noticed Armangul sitting awkwardly at the foot of the bed.

"Huh? When did you get here?"

"This morning…"

Her böle might have forgotten to close her mouth after yawning or perhaps this was her preferred mode of contemplation, but she sat there pondering, her mouth agape, for quite a while before she said, "Oh…"

She didn't actually say anything, she simply let the sound come out of her open mouth. Then she went out of the room and, after a decent amount of time passed, came back, still in her undies. "Let's go have tea," she mumbled or maybe she didn't; in any case, she jerked her head to gesture toward the door.

Her cousin's name was Turargul, and she was two years younger than Armangul. When Turargul graduated from high school, she began pestering her family by insisting that she go to college and become a lawyer.

"What do lawyers do?" Turargul's mother had inquired.

"Dinara's older sister is a lawyer; she makes tons of money!" Turargul replied.

At the time, Armangul neither understood nor asked what kind of profession it was, but she wondered if it was in any way related to Laura, the only Russian woman in their aul. Turar meant "stand by" in Kazakh, and Turargul had justified her name by standing by her promise and moving to Astana. Turargul indeed!

The next day, Armangul went with Turargul to find herself a job. When they arrived at the unemployment registration office, they had to get in a long, seemingly endless line. Turargul stepped out to have a smoke, and two women standing behind them immediately jumped the line. Armangul made no attempt to stop them. When Turargul came back reeking of cigarette smoke, she immediately ruined the two women's short-lived joy by making a scene.

"Ainalaayn, don't yell, I have a weak heart. If I pass out, you'll be the one to blame!" said one of the women, trying to defend herself. She took a pack of aspirin from her bag, threw a couple of tablets in her mouth, and stayed right where she was.

Armangul was tired of waiting. Even waiting for cows to come home for their evening milking was bliss compared to this. It took her all day to reach the door of the first room, but she came out with her hopes shattered. She imagined her hope as a young woman with a long braid, and this braid had just been chopped off. Lady Hope flipped the stump of her braid back over her shoulder, shot a glance at her, and took off. "I'm leaving," said Armangul to her böle.

"Astana is beautiful," she added, these being the only meaningful words that she had uttered since her arrival to the city.

"The guys here are handsome too!" Turargul responded.

Armangul smiled timidly.

"Let's go. We'll wear beautiful dresses, put on makeup, go to a restaurant. We'll catch ourselves some cute guys."

Armangul said nothing. In her mind's eye, she saw Lady Hope with her chopped, blonde-dyed hair turn and gaze at her.

2016

TO HELL WITH POETS

"A rrrousing poet... A rrroaring poet... A revered poet from the farrraway Atyrau... Itbai!"

The toastmaster had barely finished blaring the announcement when the poet seized the microphone from his hand and marched to the center of the room.

The top of his head glinted in the light of the restaurant's chandeliers, calling to mind the glazed surface of a lake surrounded by grassy shores. He proceeded to read a long-winded epic, pumping his fist and stomping his foot. After a while, the wedding guests began to grow bored of the performance. The women moved closer to each other and chatted among themselves. The husbands of the bride's sisters, too, good-natured and vodka-loving, formed their own little circle. Eltai dozed off in the back of the room. When he woke up, Itbai was still speaking. The DJ put on his headphones and withdrew into a world of his own. The only person listening to the poet was the meek-faced Oryngul, who was sitting in the far corner of the room. "These fools will never understand poetry," she said to herself, frowning. But she wasn't sure exactly what it was that she herself understood. The roaring voice of the poet made her tremble, sending goosebumps all over her body and bringing tears to her eyes. She felt she was born for poetry; she had been writing poems since she was a kid—for her mother, neighbors, teachers, relatives, even the egg she stumbled upon once in a chicken coop. The egg poem, which she had titled "A Life," was, in her opinion, a masterpiece:

> There's life in you, hard-shell egg.
> Make the most of it.
> In a moment, I'll smash you to pieces.
> I'll have you over easy.

She never took her eyes off the poet during the evening. She, too, wanted to step into the middle of the room and read a couple of her own poems, but she wasn't comfortable doing so with her uncle there, drinking at one of the nearby tables. Nevertheless, she managed to meet the poet later and exchange a few words with him. Out of the pocket of his cotton shirt, dotted with beads of sweat, Itbai produced a business card and handed it to Oryngul. The card was damp, and she pressed it against her cheek.

When she finally got a chance to visit the city, she decided to find Itbai. After taking an inordinate amount of time to think about what she'd say to him, she finally dialed his number. Itbai didn't make her wait long. He got Oryngul into his black Lada Samara, which he had bought on credit, and drove along the bumpy roads towards the Ural River.

"Read me one of your poems!" he demanded when they sat down on one of the benches along the embankment. She played a mournful dombyra kui on her phone and read "A Life" out loud with a rather grave expression on her face. After a moment of contemplation, Itbai said:

"Not a bad poem. The most important thing is that you've got heart. And you know what a poem is. Those country hicks will never understand that. You and I, we tower head and shoulders above them!"

His words moved Oryngul to tears. But she held them back, afraid that her smudged makeup would scare him away.

"You've come to the right person. You've got courage, you've got heart, and most importantly, you're a poet! I'll put you on the map. I'll get you published in newspapers and journals. The whole country will see what a wonderful poet you are!"

When Oryngul heard these words, she couldn't hold her emotions back anymore. She let the tears flow. Itbai began looking something up on his phone.

"Do you recognize this professor?" he asked, showing her a contact in his phone. "How about this writer? This poet has been on television a lot." He went on to show her the names of some very well-known people. "If you recognize them, you know what this means. I'm in touch with everyone. I'll get your foot in the door. All it takes is a word from me. You and I, we've got heart. We can fall in love. And those country hicks... Ah, who cares about them!"

Oryngul momentarily imagined herself speaking on television. Hoping to become famous someday, she had secretly practiced giving interviews. If someone asked her to name a cherished mentor who had guided her in her poetic journey and nurtured her interest in the art, she had planned to tell them about her elementary school teacher. She decided against that idea. Right next to her, Itbai stood, towering like a mountain.

"Tomorrow, we'll submit your poem to a local paper! Let's meet at three o'clock."

As he turned to leave, he said, "Let me kiss you on the mouth."

On the mouth! She'd heard that poets were bold. She didn't dare push him away; a kiss seemed a charming gesture worthy of a poet. The most important thing was that poets could feel deeply, that they had hearts. She closed her eyes. When Itbai's face approached hers, the brim of his hat bumped against her forehead and slid upwards, revealing his shiny scalp and releasing a shower of dandruff flakes, which alighted like flies on Oryngul's face. It was a charming gesture worthy of a poet.

They met again the next day. Trailing behind Itbai like a dog, she followed him into a tall building. He went into one of the rooms where he talked to one of the editors and then called her in.

"We must clear the eye of the spring to let it flow! Let's help a young talent soar!" Itbai said to the paper editor with great passion. The editor seemed like a nice man; he read her poem and smiled.

"We can definitely fix it," he said with a nod.

When they came out of the building, Itbai changed his demeanor.

"Didn't I tell you that this old man knows what's what? Yes, I did. Didn't I tell you that I'll get your poem in? Yes, I did. Now, if you do what I tell you, tomorrow I'll get you invited to appear on TV. I will show you that a precious gem like you doesn't have to stay buried at the bottom of a river," he said.

The afternoon was so hot that the sky seemed to be on the verge of flipping and falling on the earth. They got into Itbai's sweltering black car and drove to a multistory apartment building. Itbai began to mumble something about his feelings for her. It wasn't Oryngul's looks that he fell for but her talent, he said, adding that he liked her very much and was now in a wretched state. Now and then, he snuck in the lines from Muqaghali Maqataev's poems as if they were his own. The two of them went into the building. The short-term rental apartment smelled of stale cigarette smoke and soiled linen. There were large sneaker footprints on the dirty, worn rug. Someone must have left in a hurry, she thought. Before she was able to see the rest of the apartment, Itbai pulled her into his arms and led her to bed. A little later, she opened her eyes to find herself being kneaded like sweet roll dough beneath the heavy, sweaty Itbai. He closed his eyes and roared with pleasure. Finally, he went limp and rolled off her. A pungent stench of sweat reached her nostrils, bringing her out of a daze. She looked up at the ceiling and saw a broken chandelier with exposed wiring. "Why even bother with a chandelier?" she wondered.

She had a chuckle when she saw her poem in a local newspaper the next day. It was titled "A Life" and had her name beneath it, but she didn't recognize any of the lines. The friendly editor didn't disappoint them and had diligently revised her poem. "To hell with poets and poetry!" cried Oryngul. From that day on, whenever anyone spoke of poetry, she pictured the broken chandelier and remembered the sickening stench of sweat.

2017

TO HELL WITH POETS, PART TWO

Itbal sat in his car, waiting for riders near the bus stop. He was intent on making up the money he'd spent in a cafeteria for a group of young wannabe poets from the Quill literary club. The same old taxi job.

Suddenly, the rear door of his car flung open, then slammed shut, and a girl with disheveled hair materialized in the back. A sweet scent of perfume mixed with the pungent odor of cigarettes filled the car.

"To Privokzal'nyi for five hundred!" said the girl.

"I wish you wouldn't blacken your young lungs with smoke, darling," Itbai said, smiling, but when he glanced in the rearview mirror, his breath caught and he became tongue-tied. A strange mixture of anxiety, surprise, and joy arose in the pit of his stomach. His scalp began to sweat. If you are wondering how on earth I know about the beads of moisture popping on top of his head, let me remind you that Itbai is bald.

"Oryngul?" he said with astonishment. Oryngul abruptly stopped chomping on her gum and directed her attention to him. She squinted her eyes adorned with long, fake eyelashes and contemplated him for a minute.

"Ahh... Muqaghali?" she said with a twisted smile.

"My little crow, sweetheart, I've looked for you everywhere," Itbai replied, looking dreamily at her image in the rearview mirror. A veil, or rather spider web, of sadness came over his eyes.

"I was desperate when you disappeared," he said with a pained expression on his face. He stroked his chest pocket, which contained a leather wallet with a couple of small bills.

I'm going to interject here with a bit of gossip about Oryngul. These days, working as a hairdresser at one of the city's beauty salons, Oryngul had a decent life and income. She hadn't exactly been raking in money by trimming hair. Using only half of the forty tricks she had up her sleeve, she'd been earning her keep by kissing the foreheads of old, fat cats. Not that I'm much of a gossiper.

"Yes, I'm that old patron of yours, dear," Itbai said, feeling all soft inside. He was about to read one or two of his poems, but, sensing a change in the once-impressionable Oryngul, he held his tongue.

"How are things with you?" she asked after popping a bubble with her gum.

"The local college is letting me start a club to mentor some young poets. This old man had been clearing the eye of the same old spring."

"Huh, that many springs out there?" Oryngul said as she twisted her bright red lips into a sneer. Anxious Itbai tried to think of a way, any way, to lure Oryngul back into his arms and, sensing the opportunity slipping away, began to feel despondent.

"Did you find a job? Do you have enough money? If you need any help, let me know, don't feel shy," he ventured. At the sound of "help," Oryngul's attitude instantly changed.

"Help actually wouldn't hurt," she said, putting on a soft smile and looking almost friendly. Itbai's innocent heart almost exploded.

"If you need help... Give me a minute, dear. I have this toastmaster guy who owes me three thousand tenge. Let me call him; I'll get the money from him and give it to you," he said, reaching for his phone and starting to dial someone's number.

"Three thousand tenge? Bahaha..." Oryngul laughed, throwing her head back. Then she wiped the grin off her face and spat out her gum. The gum flew towards the center console and plopped on the face of the tape recorder emitting the soft sound of the sacred Kazakh dombyra. Oryngul yanked the door open, hurtled herself out of the car, and yelled, "Buy yourself some gas for your three thousand tenge!" as she pressed her high heels into the asphalt.

"Darling, wait," he said, hurrying to get out of his seat. Just then, the girl who had just a moment ago been standing on the other side of the car, suddenly appeared by his side. She flipped her middle finger out and brought it to Itbai's nose.

How could a fingernail be this long? Bright-red, as though dipped in blood, and pointed like a spear, the fingernail seemed to pierce his heart. All his hopes, dreams, feelings, and desires turned to ashes in his mouth as he plopped back into the driver's seat.

How could a fingernail be this long?

2018

TO HELL WITH SINGERS

The singer wearing a shapan robe trimmed with the red fox fur was without a doubt a virtuoso. When he sang "Balqadisha," sending the deep, mournful sounds soaring into the air, some of the women at the wedding toi cursed the long-dead heroine of the song: "What a pighead this Balqadisha must be to make this prince among men bawl like that!" After the performance, the smiling singer, drunk with the sounds of rapturous applause and shouts of approval, wiped his sweat-drenched temples with the fox's tail and, making sure to express his gratitude to the audience, put his hand on his chest and bowed. "May your art flourish!" cheered the bride and groom's relatives, friends and coworkers. They showered him with cash, which he tucked into his fur-trimmed shapan pockets. The pockets had been intentionally made deep.

The waitress Asemgul couldn't take her eyes off the singer. Her hands shook as she held the teapot, and she accidentally poured tea on the bared shoulder of a yellow-haired, middle-aged woman. The woman's dress was so tight that her breasts spilled over the top like a swollen, over-proofed dough.

"Argh, you snotnose!" the woman cried, her voice rising above the accolades bestowed on the singer.

Asemgul ran to the bathroom and sobbed in front of the mirror. After a long day on her feet that involved putting up with nasty women and pretty girls fussing and yelling at her, all she earned was two thousand tenge. If she had been born a singer like that man in the fur-trimmed shapan, she would have been the flower of the flock at this wedding toi, wearing a colorful dress, her pockets stuffed with money. She glanced in the mirror. Her squinty eyes, puffy from crying, and her stubby, dripping nose made it obvious to her that the realm of singers was currently out of her reach.

Suddenly, she heard the familiar beautiful voice crooning a line from "Balqadisha," "If eighty girls came strolling by..." The singer came in and stood next to her. He had apparently taken his shapan off and was now wearing a white shirt and pants.

"Why are you crying? What is your name?"

"Asemgul."

"Asemgul... Asemgul..." he murmured and, unable to recall a song dedicated to a girl with her name, shook his head. "Don't leave before the toi ends," he said and before she was able to respond, grabbed from his pocket a few bills stained with the sweat and filth of strangers, pressed them onto Asemgul's palm, and left.

How does one go about trapping a sparrow? One lures it with scraps of food. Asemgul, however, hadn't had time to ponder sparrows or snares. She was only a second-year student at a pedagogical college.

When the toi ended, the performers had begun to quibble with each other.

"Looks like you got more money than Saken."

"No, I didn't make that much."

"I'm ten thousand tenge behind Saken." Their habit of always comparing their earnings to Saken's was proof of his reputation within their circles. Proud and jubilant just a moment ago, the artsmen now looked sullen. After gathering half-emptied bottles from each table, they mixed the leftover booze and drank it, vigorously gnawing on half-eaten drumsticks between swigs.

Asemgul stood at the entrance to the banquet hall waiting for Saken. He soon arrived, and she followed him to his car, which was loaded with dombyras, guitars, microphones, and even a feathered saukele headdress. She got in and rode beside him. It didn't occur to her to ask where they were going. He brought her to a dorm room that was as small as a tit's nest.

"I'll sing for you," Saken said once they were inside. At the end of the singing, Asemgul received her first kiss.

"What if mom finds out? She'll kill me," she whispered, but her voice was drowned out by Saken's unsavory groan. Yielding to the mixed feelings of curiosity and fear, she was only half-aware of what was happening. When it was over, she rubbed her thighs, numb from being pressed and squashed by Saken's heavy body.

"We'll get married, right?" she ventured. Saken didn't respond. Getting out of bed, he nearly stumbled over a dombyra lying face up on the floor and kicked it away. The dombyra made an odd whining noise when it landed in a corner of the room. As if echoing the sound, the bed creaked as Asemgul turned over on her stomach and began to whimper.

"I'll give you some more money so you can buy a nice dress," said Saken, but she didn't hear him.

2017

BOARBAI

"Tell you what," he said, his jaws moving vigorously up and down as he chewed on a piece of meat. He stabbed a slice of cucumber with a fork and tossed it in his mouth, biting into it with a loud crunch. Soon, the cucumber slice was on its way to his gut.

"Here's the thing. I've wanted to talk to you about this for a while, but those yapping bitches are always hanging around you and I can't catch a moment alone with you."

"They aren't yapping bitches. They're my friends."

"Well, they will be someone's bitches one day. Ba-ha-ha…" He shook with laughter. A bit of dill was stuck between his front teeth.

Aibike looked away. She took a sip of cold water to suppress her revulsion. Boarbai swallowed, glowering at a lipstick stain on the rim of her glass, and continued, "Speaking of those bitches… They've got nothing on you. You're the prettiest."

Just look at him sweet-talking, she thought.

"Your food will get cold. Give it to me if you're not going to eat it. You women never appreciate good food." He reached for a chicken drumstick and, holding it tightly as if it was going to run away from him, began to gnaw at it.

"I've wanted to tell you this for a while... I like you. Did you get the gift I sent?"

Aibike couldn't help but smile, remembering a pair of hand-knit socks that were clearly meant for a person with size-ten feet. His mother must have knitted them for Boarbai.

"Yes, I did."

"Put them on. They'll keep you warm."

He picked the last of the meat off the drumstick and dropped it on to his plate.

"I'm going to marry you!" he blurted out.

Wow, this guy doesn't waste time! Aibike thought. She struggled to come up with a response and, in the end, decided to remain silent. Boarbai smiled at her, evidently interpreting her silence as a tacit agreement.

"I knew you had a thing for me! I know, it's hard for a girl to say these things, so I thought I'd help you out." She tried to remember if she'd ever heard him use the word "girl" before.

His face grew serious and thoughtful. After picking his teeth with a toothpick, he inserted it into his nostril and winced. Then he sent it spinning into the air with a flick of his fingers. The toothpick landed on one of the tables nearby.

Boarbai pulled out his phone and began fumbling with it. His large, stubby fingers kept pressing two or three buttons at once, and it took him some time to dial a number.

"Yep, all done. See you in half an hour," he said briefly and hung up.

His sunburnt, chapped skin was lighter in the creases of his face. He spoke again.

"We grew up together. You don't have an older brother, so I always tried to protect you from bullies."

Aibike was baffled. How was she to know that she'd end up having a conversation on such a paramount subject with Boarbai, who had dropped in at her dorm today to deliver a message and some food and treats from her mother? She didn't know how to tell him that his proposal was completely inappropriate and that the thought of starting a family, let alone with him, had not even crossed her mind. She decided to keep quiet for now, but after this meeting she was going to make sure he never saw her again.

"Boarbai agha, it's getting late. I should be going."

"Well now, I don't want your mother to be upset with me, thinking I sent you back to the dorms alone at night. I'll get you there in no time. My nephew's waiting outside in his car."

Eager to get away from him at any cost, Aibike agreed. This is the last time you'll be seeing me, Boarbai! she said to herself. Looking quite pleased with himself, Boarbai strode toward the door when a waitress' ringing voice called out: "Would you like the check, agha?" He handed her a five-thousand-tenge bill and said: "Keep the change! Treat yourself at the expense of a future bridegroom!" He winked and let out a snorting chuckle.

"Get us to the sleeping quarters, nephew!" he said as soon as they got into the car, chuckling again for no apparent reason.

The car sped along the asphalt road, glistening in the drizzling rain. They headed toward the edge of the town, taking the side roads. When the car pulled onto the highway where the bus to her remote village ran, Aibike's heart began beating wildly. She began to shriek and bawl. Boarbai squeezed her thin shoulders as she thrashed and kicked in his rigid embrace.

"There, there, be a good girl," he said, snorting with laughter. Her glance fell on his face, illuminated momentarily by the headlights of an oncoming car. He was grinning, and she could see the bit of dill still stuck in his teeth.

2016

THE APRICOT TREE BLOOMS

The sun rose early. It was beating down on my face when I woke up. Worried that I was late for school, I kicked off the thin camel wool blanket and leapt out of bed. The blanket was becoming too small for me: in the morning, I'd always find my feet sticking out of it. I hurried toward the kitchen which smelled of a delightful mixture of samovar smoke and the strongly brewed tea. I found my mother and father having breakfast. I came in wearing my usual underwear, but this time my mom glared at me.

"Why aren't you dressed? Were you chased by raiders?" she said. As I turned around, I heard her grumbling to herself, "Does she have any sense of shame, this girl?"

I couldn't have become a woman overnight, could I? I was only finishing sixth grade. Still, it might be inappropriate for a girl in sixth grade to show up in front of her father in her underwear, her hair disheveled. I still felt like my dad's little girl. He was very fond of me, and he still liked to sniff my forehead, rubbing his bristly chin against it, when he was feeling affectionate.

Yesterday, I noticed the girls in my class whispering over some letters which looked to be written by older boys. I wondered why no one had written to me. I felt jealous and thought about telling on the girls to the teacher. I had lost track of time, pondering all this, and was startled to hear my mother yelling, "Hurry up, girl, you'll be late for school!" I quickly got dressed.

Lately, I hadn't been letting mom do my hair because she braided it too tightly. It didn't look pretty. It stuck out like a leather plait, slapping against my back when I walked. I spat on my hand, using the saliva to make my bangs shine and lie flat. I reminded myself to ask dad to buy me hair gel later.

Outside, an apricot tree was in bloom, and its flower buds gave off a subtle sweet aroma. My dad started his motorcycle. The smell of gasoline overpowered the delicate scent of the flowers. I climbed onto the motorcycle and wrapped my arms around dad's waist. Pressing my face lightly into his gray jacket, I inhaled the familiar smell of pungent sweat. We rode to school, filling the street with blue smoke. The wind was blowing hard, and I could smell the saliva I had smeared on my bangs. I shouldn't have done that. It would be embarrassing if that seventh-grader N, who pulled on my braid every day and called it a "goat's tail," figured out I shined my hair with spit. Lately, whenever I saw N, I would freeze, and my heart beat fast. Why was I afraid of him?

2016

ICE CREAM

Occasionally touching the sticky glaze smeared above his lips with his tongue, Yerkesh shared his extraordinary tales about ice cream.

"I'm telling you, there's nothing that compares with its sweetness. When you lick it, it feels like ice is pouring into your mouth. It chills your tongue, and when you swallow, the ice cream slides down into your stomach, and your chest starts to feel really cold." He traced a path from his throat to his belly with his dark, sunburnt hand. Unable to imagine the flavor as vividly as Yerkesh did, we wistfully followed his hand with our eyes.

"Ah, so sweet," he murmured, closing his eyes and licking the last of the sticky ice cream residue above his mouth with the tip of his tongue. We gazed reverently at the viscous glaze beneath his nose, having given up on imagining the taste of the ice cream. That day, we returned home, secretly fantasizing of traveling to the city and being left alone in an ice cream shop.

Every time I ate something sweet, I couldn't help but wonder if ice cream was even more delicious. I envied the relatives who occasionally came to visit us from the city: they were lucky people who had tasted ice cream.

Finally, the day arrived when I was told that I'd be traveling to the city with my father. Feeling jubilant as though I were the one slashing a sacrificial white camel's stomach open before a celebration, I broke the china piggy bank where I kept the change I'd been saving up. Some of the coins had blackened from being thrown into their dark prison for too long. I polished them by rubbing them on the high-pile carpet and put them in my pocket. I was ready for my mission to taste ice cream.

Dragging its belly across the ground, the groaning old bus had finally reached the bazaar at the edge of the city and spat out its passengers. My father tightly gripped my sweaty little hand in his giant palm to make sure he didn't lose me. I looked about, turning my head left and right, as I walked along. The bazaar, which I imagined as a festive, colorful public square, turned out to be a place full of people rushing to and fro in search of something, beggars stretching out their withered palms, and drudges carrying heavy loads on their backs. The edge of the bazaar was taken over by old women. An elderly Kazakh lady wearing a grimy floral scarf whose color had faded in the sun was selling qūrt balls, made of dried sour yogurt. The dust raised by many people's feet settled on the pile of white qūrt in her open sack. Her goods looked as unclean as the scarf on her head.

Next to her sat an old Russian woman selling dried fish. Once in a while, she chased off the flies crawling on the fish with her fan. But even as she shooed them away, she seemed to regret it as though she had grown fond of them; if they weren't there, she might have been bored to death by her slow business.

A lady selling beautiful flowers on delicate stems looked hopefully into passersby's eyes. A pretty flower planted in a clay pot was the loveliest thing I'd come across at the bazaar. Its gently quivering head entranced me. Suddenly, someone in the swarm of people rushing by grazed the pot with their foot, and it fell to the ground. The flower vendor quickly gathered the scattered soil, put it back into the pot, and lodged the flower in it. The flower had no roots.

I mentally counted the coins in my pocket and realized I had enough to buy two portions of ice cream. I knew that dad couldn't afford to spend any money on me. Before we left, my mother had given him a piece of paper that listed the things he had to buy along with their exact cost. "It's been five years since I've worn a new dress, yet that blue car gets a new part every month," my mother grumbled, but my dad, who pampered his car by constantly greasing, adjusting, and replacing its components, was still determined to spend whatever money would be left over from our shopping today on the new car parts. He didn't say anything to me, but I knew his plans.

We had passed through the peddler market and were getting closer to the part of the bazaar where they sold ice cream. By then, my father had found and bought all the things we needed. A disabled man leaning on a cane, whose face was streaked with profuse amounts of wrinkles, held his hand out. My father threw him a couple of coins. The man's eyes lit up with hope as he thanked him. I figured one portion of ice cream might be enough for me and, hoping to see even more joy in the man's eyes, decided to give him some of my money. I had meant to drop only one of the coins that had turned damp in my sweaty palms, but instead four or five of them fell jingling into his box. I froze, not daring to bend over to take my coins back when my father tugged at my hand, dragging me along with him, and, unable to stop him, I melded into the crowd of people barreling through as they stepped on one another's heels.

My father didn't even notice that I'd given money to the beggar man. What was I to do? I was so upset I could barely hold back my tears. I kept angrily wiping them away, but my bitterness about missing out on ice cream turned into a hot bile that surged upwards and filled my eyes. Bleary-eyed, I began to stumble. My father must have noticed a change in my grip or else got tired; he too slowed down. He looked dubiously into my puffy eyes, and I said sobbing, "Iiice creeeaaam…" I'd been tired and unhappy, and the river of tears came streaming down my face. He must have anticipated something much worse because he said casually, "Oh, oh, ice cream!" Then he laughed and turned toward a woman standing next to a white freezer.

Who knew that ice cream that I'd dreamt of so much, that had given me a taste of grief, and that was to remain the stuff of fairytales to some of the kids in the aul, would be so easy to get my hands on? We bought not just one but three cones of ice cream. The plump lady in an apron seemed so friendly and her ice cream so wonderful! I quit sobbing and, looking happily at my father, licked the top of my ice cream. It was just like Yerkesh said: it melted on your tongue, leaving a deliciously sweet taste.

When the bazaar began closing, we too headed out toward home. I saw the beggar man standing near the entrance, but this time his arms and legs seemed to be fine. His greasy cane was tucked under his armpit and he belched as he drank the sparkling water out of a bottle.

2017

THE BROWN RAM LAMB

It was the middle of August. We had been spending less time running barefoot outside and begun switching our sun-burnt selves back into school mode. Wondering where all the pens and pencils had gone since the beginning of summer break and failing to find a scrap of paper after searching everywhere, we finally set to scribbling down a list of clothes and supplies for the new school year on the inner side of an empty tea carton. We needed money to buy all the things on our list.

The next day, our father came home with a livestock trader and let him into the qora where the animals were kept. When my younger brother heard our parents say, "We'll have to sell a sheep," he pricked up his ears and headed towards the qora too. "I hope they don't sell my brown ram lamb," he muttered. Their fat tails trembling and their eyes averted from the peering human stares, a dozen sheep timidly huddled in one of the qora corners. After walking around, squeezing, and cupping their tails in his hands, the trader lingered near the brown ram lamb. I looked at my brother and saw that his eyes turned the size of his palms as he sensed an injustice was about to take place. The trader had barely said, "I'll buy this one!" when he began bawling. He pressed his face into the sheep's red-brown fleece reeking of wool wax and cried loudly, unwilling to let the sheep go, and my dad put his arms around him, hoping to pick him up and take him away. The bewildered ram lamb began bleating hoarsely in the midst of this commotion.

"You'll buy new shoes tomorrow. Come on, stop crying!" I comforted my brother.

"I don't want them," he said desolately. His face, damp with tears and sweat, had a few brown hairs glued to it.

The brown ram lamb was sold. Occasionally wetting the tips of her fingers with saliva, my mom sat counting the money. In a corner, my brother lay sobbing with his face down and knees bent. I sat by my mother's side, fanning my face with the piece of tea carton, on which a list of school supplies was written down.

In September, my brother, sporting shiny brown leather shoes, was walking beside me to school. His grief for the brown ram lamb must have faded because he was smiling as he chattered about his friends who had grown taller over the summer.

"I like how shiny your shoes are, and they have a nice color, red-brown like your favorite ram lamb," I said carelessly. He sighed deeply and kept walking without taking his eyes off his shoes.

2017

SUPERSTITIONS

The neighbors were having a tusaukeser ceremony to celebrate their toddler's first steps. When I entered the house, I saw a group of men sitting on a rug and throwing banknotes and cards on it as they gambled. My dad sat nearby, leaning on a pillow by his side and watching them with interest.

"Why isn't he playing? He probably has no money," I thought. "When I grow up, I'll make a lot of money so he can play cards with these men." My younger brother had said these same words last fall, when at some toi, a group of drunk men got into a fight, and my dad, who never missed an event where "firewater" was passed around, ended up with a bloody lip. "When I grow up, I'll be a martial artist. I'll beat up the guys who hurt dad," he said then.

When I had enough of watching the card game, I went to find my mom in the kitchen. Half a dozen women, whose heads occasionally appeared amid the clouds of steam from the pots with boiling meat, were loudly and all at once talking about Sulushash, who didn't come to the tusaukeser party.

"Last year she wore a brown coat, and this winter a dark blue one. We'd wondered where she'd gotten the money for those; now we know how they made their living."

"Has the stolen money ever brought anyone any good?"

"There were always fruits and candy on her dastarkhan."

"How long is he going to be in jail for?"

"It's not an easy job to embezzle money from a huge company."

"He can't be doing less than ten years."

I gathered from their conversation that Sulushash's husband was put in jail for stealing money. Their son Nurdaulet used to pass by our house several times a day to show off his brand-new bicycle with shiny wheels. I wondered how all this made him feel.

The tusaukeser ceremony began. Ala jip—a strap made of braided white and black yarn—was tied around the child's ankles, and then a taqiyah-wearing grandpa cut it with scissors.

"Don't ever cross ala jip!"

"May you never make a false step!"

"Grow to be a good man!" people in the room spoke all at once as they exclaimed traditional wishes. I whispered to my mom sitting near me, "Mom, what does it mean to not cross ala jip?"

"It means: don't steal, don't take what another person had worked hard for. It's a ritual done with the hope that a child will grow honest and fair." Her words made me think about Nurdaulet's dad locked up in prison.

"Does that mean Nurdaulet's father didn't have his ala jip strap cut when he was little?"

Instead of pondering my question, my mom reproached me.

"Next time, don't eavesdrop on grown-ups' conversations," she said, smacking me across my ear.

On the way home, we saw Sulushash-apa. She was beating a red silk rug outside her house. My mom's eyes would normally light up whenever she saw something pretty, but this time she didn't even look at the rug. She acknowledged Sulushash with a quick glance and kept going. Perhaps she sensed that people were gossiping about her or maybe she was simply not in a good mood, but Sulushash didn't turn to look at us and, swinging her arm ever wider, went on forcefully beating the rug. The sound of the carpet beater hitting against the rug still rang in the air when we got home. They should have used ala jip, I kept thinking.

II

In early winter, my dad often joined other village men to go fishing in the sea. He then made money by selling the fish. When his earnings were good, he brought us sweets from a local shop. He probably put them in the same bag where he kept his fishing tools and supplies because they always smelled of fish. Sometimes there were fish scales stuck to the edges of the bills that he pressed onto my mom's palm.

But lately, dad hadn't been bringing any sweets. He hadn't caught any fish. My superstitious mom said, "An evil eye was put on his hands," and tied a red string to his fishing rod. "We must change the bag too. It's been blocking the good catch," she said and threw the withered bag, dried up from the fish slime it was often drenched with, into the burning wood stove.

She rummaged the trunk and found a red schoolbag I used to carry in first grade. "Your daughter's red bag is full of As. It could be a good charm. Take it. No one will care what bag you're using at sea," she said. I felt she cared more about the bag's color than about its being "full" of my good grades. On my dad's broad back my small schoolbag looked more like a pocketbook.

"May this bag bring us abundance," my mom murmured. I flashed a smile to my brother, convinced that later that day we'd be getting sweet treats on account of my bag. When my dad returned from his fishing trip in the evening, he dropped the bag carelessly by the door. There was no fish slime on it; it was squeaky-clean. Which meant that no fish was caught that day.

III

Since getting a job in construction, my dad had been coming home drunk every night. After work, he and his coworkers drank some vodka to unwind. My mom's sighs became more frequent. My brother, who missed going on motorcycle rides with dad, was unhappy too. I too felt irritated to hear him come home belting out off-key, "Ah, oh, your swinging waist, Qamazhai!" I was ashamed of him before my friends.

After spending some time studying his habits and keeping track of his sober days, my mom came to a conclusion, "I noticed that when your father wears his blue shirt, he comes home drunk." The blue shirt was the culprit of our troubles.

In the morning, as my dad got ready to go to work, I stood fidgeting by his side for a few minutes, then mumbled, "Daddy, please don't wear this blue shirt..."

"What?"

"Just don't wear it!"

I looked at my mom; her eyebrows, drawn with black pencil to replicate the ones of a famous actress, were by turns twisting and stretching. She seemed to be signaling me to hold tight to the shirt. I didn't have time to figure out when she had managed to do her eyebrows; one shirt sleeve already had my dad's arm in it. If dad left wearing the blue shirt, I knew that my mom's eyebrows would turn wintry, and she would take her anger out on me and my brother. The critical moment is upon us, I thought, not quite sure where I picked up this fancy expression. I tugged at the yet unworn sleeve and, after pulling the shirt off my dad, headed toward the door. "Hey, hey... What's up with her?" stammered my dad, but I didn't let him finish and darted outside, slamming the door behind me. His tongue hanging, our dog Aqtös rushed to catch up with me. I cried angrily as I ran. I wiped my tears with the blue shirt that had caused all the trouble in our family. The shirt smelled of sweat and vodka.

A little while later, as I drew near our house, I saw my dad walking away with a white shirt on. I was in a good mood all day, imagining dad coming home sober, having dinner with us, laughing and telling jokes, and then taking us all out for a ride on his motorcycle. My mom's eyebrows too were uncurled, and she fried some baursaks and spread a new dastarkhan on the dining table. She rolled out a körpe with ornate appliques, usually reserved for guests. Humming a song, she trimmed my brother's nails, wiped his nose with a wet towel, and brushed away his bangs.

The light of the setting sun colored my dad's white shirt yellow-red as he walked towards home. The closer he got, the more obvious it became that his step was unsteady. He was drunk again. The white shirt didn't help us.

2017

THE WARMTH

She put the pieces of dry dung into the sack, brought it into the house, opened the wood stove door, and emptied the sack into the firebox. My siblings and I had gathered the dung over the summer, often getting into fights with other kids. There was a story behind each piece of that dung. That thin whitish piece, dipped in diesel to make it ignite at once, had been produced by the cow with a broken horn that belonged to our neighbor Qambar. After finding old Qambar's cow eating the hay saved for our own cows, I chased it away, yelling, "Botflies on you and blackleg too!" and every other curse I knew. When the wet flop she'd dropped as she walked away dried up in the sun, I picked it up and placed it against the wall of our cow pen. Yes, each piece of dung had a story like that.

Baked in the summer heat, the dung crackled as it caught fire. Our brown masonry stove came alive. The blazing fire had soon heated up its mud-plastered walls, and the warmth began spreading through the house. A weathered black cast-iron pot was placed on top of the stove. My grandmother rinsed it with hot water, whispered her unfailing "Bismillah," and put a chunk of meat in it. She squinted as she glanced at the clock on the opposite wall. She then sat down with her back against the stove and retrieved a book with yellowed pages from under the körpe mat. I moved closer to her. A habitual move; in our house, words were seldom spoken, yet things still ran their course.

The brown wood stove and my grandmother were alike in that their warmth made us kids always seek them out when we were cold. The two always seemed to silently sympathize with each other: the brown stove looked lonely when my grandmother wasn't around, and she was cheerless when there was no fire in the stove. I wasn't afraid of the blizzard howling outside; it was powerless against my grandmother and the brown wood stove. It could rage and wreak havoc all around us and even try to break into our house, but it would inevitably lose its vigor and die down in the end. All the while, my grandmother and I sat with our backs against the wood stove, basking in its warmth. She put her glasses on and started reading her book in a low voice. I placed my head on her lap and began listening. To tell the truth, she didn't read to entertain or educate me; she read for her own pleasure. She couldn't read without voicing the words, but I had to get really close to hear her soft whisper. We had gotten to the middle of the book about the Great Retreat of Kazakhs from the Jungar invasion, which we had started reading yesterday. The terrible suffering of people during that time distressed my grandmother, and she kept sighing deeply and saying, "Oh, poor souls!" But I didn't know if she grieved for the characters in the book or her own generation, nearly wiped out by the great famine of the thirties that she'd sometimes tell me about.

During those quiet hours, I listened closely to the sounds of the house. There was the soft murmur of my grandmother's voice. The crackling of the fire in the wood stove. The burbling of the water in the pot. The groaning of the snowstorm outside. The wheezing sound of my breath. Suddenly, there was a teardrop on my face. Behind lenses thick as the bottom of a milk bottle, my grandmother's eyes welled up with tears, which ran down along the lines on her face and fell onto my face. But she kept reading. Her voice trembled as she whispered again, "Oh, poor souls..."

I woke up from the sweet scent of the salt-cured meat tickling my nose. The book, open on a dog-eared page, lay on the körpe, and my grandmother was busy setting the table. After spending all day out in the steppe herding sheep, my grandfather came in, his fur hat brought all the way down to his frost-touched eyebrows. In our house, all things were silently connected to each other. My grandfather rarely told us when he'd come home, but the moment he entered the house, the meal was ready and the table was already being set. And my grandmother would have read another chapter of her book.

The years passed. My grandfather died, and my grandmother moved to the regional center to live with her oldest son. The small house with the wood stove in the middle had been taken down, the soil beneath it excavated, and some other building put in its place. The gas line was installed, and children, who didn't have to collect dung anymore, grew bored and restless. The streets became littered with manure, but there was no one to pick it up and make use of it. And having become sensitive to cold weather, I'd been searching for the warmth ever since.

2016

THE COBBLER

For as long as he could remember, all he'd seen were shoe inserts and soles. His body had adjusted itself to his trade: his back hunched, he sat with his neck bent low, and his head rarely rose above his shoulders. Even his thick, horsehair eyebrows grew downward. He had a habit of sniffling and wheezing through his nose. He thought of his perpetually dripping nose as a drain for excess fluids leaking from his brain on account of his always looking downwards. When the sewing thread in his hand broke or a nail didn't go in straight, the sound of his sniffing grew more frequent. The small size of the stool his tailbone was pressed against and the way he sat on it with his knees bent comfortably revealed his short stature. As for his hair, because he always wore the old malakhai hat, soiled and falling apart at the seams, he didn't have to go to a hairdresser often. He only went when his graying hair would fall onto the nape of his neck, curl around his ear, or stick out of the malakhai. There was dirt embedded under his fingernails and inside the skin cuts and cracks in his hands. Sometimes the mold seemed to be growing on his hands. His clothes looked grimy, and he used his apron to wipe the glue off his fingers. Occasionally at the end of a work day, he was heard singing hoarsely some unrecognizable tune with unintelligible lyrics. But there weren't many people who had picked up on it.

He was a cobbler. No one knew what his name was. He made his living by fixing random passersby's shoes. He always looked at people's feet and the shoes they handed over but almost never at their faces. Whenever he spotted a shiny new pair of shoes, he entertained himself by guessing how long it would take for their owner to wear them out. If a client admired his work, he'd instantly get nervous and sweaty, his eyebrows and mouth would start twitching, and he'd look very uncomfortable. In those moments, he didn't always know what to say. Yet he'd always quickly look around to see if other people had heard him being praised for his skillfulness. He especially wished the words of appreciation to reach the ears of a fair-skinned, wide-waisted woman selling samsa in the booth next to his.

When the work was over, he came out of his booth and locked the door. Though he wasn't hungry, he bought a samsa from the adjacent booth. He ate it standing next to the counter. The samsa seller, hastily chopping onions with her large knife, paid no attention to him, though he kept looking inside the booth as if he wanted to say something to her. Perhaps he wanted to tell her of a person who had thanked him today for wonderfully warm insoles or of a young man who had paid him extra after simultaneously patting him on the back, giving him a thumbs up, and saying, "You're a wizard!"

After finishing up his samsa, he wiped his mouth with a dirty cloth retrieved from his pocket, and, looking down and scrunching his face in an effort to smile, said "Thank you!" When he heard the soft-voiced samsa seller ask, "You're still here?" a feeling of warmth rushed, like a gulp of hot tea, from his throat down to his stomach. "Yes, I made good money today, and I finished all the orders early," he wanted to say. By then, several minutes had passed since the question was posed, and, realizing the awkward timing of his response, he remained silent.

His shoulders hunched, he began to hesitantly walk away, then turned around and looked at the booth's front window, where the woman's forearms were rapidly moving as she continued to prep the onions. She quickly wiped off the tears spurting from her eyes and resumed her task. A thin man in a new, oversized suit came up to the booth and began bantering with the samsa seller. If it wasn't for his unkempt, run-down shoes, he might be taken for a manager at some firm or one of those bustling individuals always found by the side of local politicians. The samsa seller, her face red from the heat of the oven where the pastry was baked, might have thought so too. She laughed, sticking her head out of her booth's window. Not used to smiling, the cobbler too stretched his mouth in a grin. Who he grinned at or why was not clear.

On the bus ride home, he listened to other people's conversations. Some talked about the recent shocking crime incident, others complained about high gas prices. An old woman who lived in his neighborhood was exasperated by the unpaved, perpetually mud-mired streets. Every time her voice became a little louder, she stomped on the floor of a dilapidated bus, whose insides threatened to burst and spill out any minute. The mud on her old boots hadn't been cleaned for so long that it hardened, turning into concrete. The cobbler too pursed his lips as if about to join one of these multifarious conversations. But he didn't know what to say. He made an effort to stretch the corners of his mouth into an awkward smile and immediately felt embarrassed. Worried that someone might have seen him smiling, he timidly looked up from under his eyebrows, whose occasional long, curly strands fell over his eyes. But no one at the bus was looking at him.

He finally reached a small summer house surrounded by rampantly-growing trees at the edge of a city. A black-and-white cat, who had lain by the lukewarm stove all day, stretched, sinking its claws into the wooden floor, then meowed, wrapping itself around his legs. The cobbler lit up the stove and warmed up some milk. "It would be nice if they paved the road on our street," he murmured. The cat dipped its whiskers into the milk.

2018

ONE-DAY MARRIAGE

"My son's getting married," said Roza, the hem of her dress flapping about and her shoes haphazardly worn, with her heels on the shoe counters, as she went from house to house. Some felt happy for her, saying, "Eh Allah, that sordid boy of hers was to bring her joy after all." Others wondered, "What kind of woman could have stumbled into that stutterer?"

Years ago, Roza's son Zhaqash had his head shaved, and, along with every other young man his age, rolled into a blue train car that took him to the army quarters. The rigid military discipline didn't work out for the doted-on boy who had grown up clinging to his mother's skirt. Four months later, a brown UAZ jeep showed up in the aul, and a group of soldiers holding Zhaqash up by his armpits helped him into his house. Something must have shocked him back in the military because he was now stuttering. Once in a while, he had seizures that turned his skin blue and left him unconscious. The know-it-alls insisted that he had had a good kick in the head. As for Roza, she opted not to dig into what had happened or go to court.

"I missed him so much he'd come into my dreams; I'm glad he came home early. My little baby, as long as he has his arms and legs, he'll be fine," she said, her eyes welling with tears.

It was this Zhaqash who was about to get married. A woman going from aul to aul selling golden rings and earrings struck up a friendship with Roza and, taking a liking to reserved Zhaqash, called her daughter in, and the two hit it off with each other. Zhaqash too liked the yellow-haired girl with black eyebrows, enormous eyes, and olive skin. The gold seller had adopted and raised the girl after taking her in from an orphanage where she had apparently been mistreated.

"A mother's love came to me later than to most people. I used to be really jealous of kids who had mothers. God fulfilled my wishes and gave me two mothers instead of one. My dear apa!" the girl said, embracing Roza, and none of the women in the room could hold back their tears. With her heart about to split in two and tears dripping down her chin, Roza squeezed her eyes shut, bit her lips, and nodded repeatedly.

Her new mother-in-law or qudaghi, a large woman with short red hair, three pairs of earrings in her ears, and gold teeth, sat at the tör, the seat of honor, and spoke, her voice occasionally rising to a hiss, "I'm a widow myself; my husband was stabbed one night by some city robbers. We didn't have any children. Afterwards, I made living by sweeping the front yard of an orphanage. This girl kept following me around like a lost lamb. Whenever she saw me, she'd say, "Mamatai!" and cling to me. I found out later that I looked a lot like her mother. I'd get the permission from caretakers at the orphanage and take her home with me sometimes. After I left that job, I kept thinking of the girl, and when I finally went back to see her, I found her crying because she was being harassed by the older kids. I couldn't leave her like that, so I adopted her." The women shed tears again.

After crying along with everybody, the thickset qudaghi looked tenderly with her gummed eyes at Zhaqash, sitting next to her, and said, "He is my son too. Ainalaayn, I saw the beautiful light in your eyes, and I knew I could trust my daughter to you!" She nearly shoved her nose into the grown man's ear and inhaled to show her affection, and no one thought her gesture bizarre.

"Roza, don't go all out to prepare for a wedding, I don't have a lot of spare time. Let's get them married and have the toi before I leave," she said, setting the date of the wedding.

It was long past midnight, but the loud voices of the aul women at Roza's house were not even close to winding down. They crooned, recounting the bride's and her mother's fables to each other. As they passed from one mouth to another, the fables grew more colorful and thrilling.

"Why d-d-d-don't you g-g-g-go home? It's really late," said Zhaqash, looking at the women.

A little later, he stuttered again, "T-t-t-turn the light off, the house is full of mosquit-t-t-toes."

But the steam rising from the white tea kettle that had just come off the stove made it clear that the guests wouldn't be leaving any time soon. The wide legs of Zhaqash's trousers rustled, rubbing against each other, as he paced the room. He wanted to talk to his bride, who sat looking like a doll, her headscarf sliding backwards and revealing more of her yellow-dyed hair, glimmering in the overhead light, and maybe hold her by the hand, but his heart kept bucking and leaping.

The guests finally dispersed when the stars in the sky began looking anemic.

By the time Zhaqash made up his mind to speak to his bride, the rooster, bothered by the comb that kept falling over his eyes, called for the morning azan. Dogs barked, and cows lowed. Roza emerged with a clanging pail and headed towards the cow pen. Qudaghi didn't stay idle and went round the aul selling gold. Three or four days later they had a wedding toi. Zhaqash's peers, who had married a while ago and already had several kids, were impressed.

"His woman is like a doll, and her waist looks like it would snap any minute," one of them said with fascination in his voice.

"Zhaqash the stammerer got ahead of us," joked another, his voice tinted with jealousy.

"Taking Zhaqash's mother-in-law as a wife wouldn't be so bad either," laughed the third. Though the red dog of envy kept clawing at their insides, deep down, they wished him well.

"Well, God gives each man according to his intentions. Whenever we asked Zhaqash for help, he never said 'no,'" they said, this time looking serious.

"You know what happens during the tamarisk-cutting season? We take turns and help each other out to get the job done. By the time Zhaqash's turn comes, it would be snowing, and we'd always find a reason not to go out to help him, but Zhaqash never complained," said a guy who was Zhaqash's age.

"Yeah, whatever you say, he responds with 'sure' and rushes to help you. He never changes."

"If you tell him, 'Forget your wedding, let's go get this or that done,' he'll join you without thinking," someone laughed.

Zhaqash looked sharp in a white shirt and black suit. When the song dedicated to fathers was played, Roza danced with the new mother-in-law. Those present at the toi shed their tears again, mourning the untimely passing of Zhaqash's late father. "He didn't get to have the joy of seeing his only son married."

There was an outpouring of well wishes and a wonderful feeling of genuine camaraderie all throughout the toi. Beneath a white veil, the bride's gray eyes sparkled like quicksilver.

When Roza woke up early in the morning, she wanted to get the samovar going, but then, reluctant to spoil her brand-new daughter-in-law's enthusiasm, stayed in bed. In her younger days, she didn't like it when her mother-in-law got up before her; when it happened, she felt guilty and anxious and would trip over her own feet all day. She smiled to herself, remembering her own silliness. Let the daughter-in-law feel herself at home and get used to doing things around the house, she thought.

The clock, however, kept clicking its tongue and striking out the time by the handful, so she finally got out of bed. She went to the room in the back where the qudaghi was put up but found the room empty and her bed unmade. She then came to her son's bedroom and, hesitant to open the door, stood in front of it for some time. She remembered the first night after her own wedding and smiled again.

By afternoon they learned that the qudaghi and her daughter were seen boarding an early-morning bus to the city. They didn't leave with empty hands; they took with them the wedding dress, the money gifted by the guests, and the gold given in exchange for a traditional "viewing" of the bride. Roza couldn't find her dentures kept in a glass on a kitchen table either. There were a couple of gold-plated teeth in it. She couldn't even bite her lip in frustration.

When yet another villager's head popped up above her fence, followed by "Have your hands grown longer now that you have a daughter-in-law?" Roza didn't know what to say. What would Zhaqash do when he woke up after having danced all night with his friends? In the meantime, two women who had by then managed to sell the stolen goods, sat at a city cafe and, clinking their beer glasses, hatched their next plans.

2018

IN SEARCH OF A CHARACTER

The taxi is racing along the streets of Astana, and the splendid buildings graze the corner of my eye before disappearing behind. As soon as the doors to the airport building open, the velvety scent of coffee hits my nose and settles in its depths. I look up to find Atyrau among the quickly-changing destinations on a blue screen. I have one hour before my flight. Once again, I'll return home without a new character. My quest in search of a hero or heroine for my next story had ended unsuccessfully. Should I pluck someone out of this suitcase-lugging crowd and throw, like a lasso, someone else's fate onto their necks? Should I write about the man with oily cheeks, shiny forehead, and silvery hair who sat next to me in the business-class section on my earlier flight here? We didn't say a word to each other; he never took his eyes off the paper he was reading, his chin tucked into the collar of his thick blue sweater. Or should my character be the flight attendant, a young lady with a sharp face seemingly cast of bronze, slick hair pulled back into a tight bun, and wide eyes with whites so pristine that love and goodness seemed to pour out of them whenever she looked at me? Why didn't I talk to the porter who greeted me at the entrance to my hotel, then gently took my rattling suitcase consisting only of a pair of high heels and a silk dress, and stood straight as an arrow while we rode the elevator? And the man in a checkered shirt cutting up a thin sausage with the tip of his silver knife at breakfast and slowly chewing it as his cloudy gray eyes beneath his thick, curved brows darted furtive glances in my direction—what kind of character could he turn into? What conversation did I have last night at a restaurant with the guy who I clinked the wine-filled glasses with and who resembled someone I knew or perhaps didn't resemble anyone yet whose face I had difficulty remembering the next morning? The thoughts wear out my brain, which hasn't yet recovered from the toxic sludge of last night's wine. My head begins spinning. The city of Astana, just as dazzling at night as it was during the day, entranced me and made me forget my quest.

I feel the tiny capillaries in my sleep-deprived eyes fill with blood and my eyeballs about to burst. When I squeeze my eyes shut, tears flow out of their corners. Will some casual observer decide I am crying because I am sad about parting with my lover?

When did I cry last? I remember the day a Whatsapp message had showed up on my phone, "A wind from Atyrau is blowing and it seems to have brought your scent with it. Come to Almaty!" and immediately another app had announced that my bank account was replenished. I habitually shoved a dress and a pair of shoes into an empty suitcase and with my big curly hair whooshing about and my suitcase's wheels whirring, flew out the door.

The gaping mouths of empty beer bottles crowding the paper-cluttered desk made the bleak, unkempt room even more gloomy.

"Ainalaayn, you're here!" he said, his body leaping forward even before he was able to fully get up from his seat. As he pulled me towards himself, bringing my face closer to his shirt smelling of tobacco and beer, I noticed that his untidy hair was overgrown and his hardened yellowish fingernails were too long.

"My novel's characters have been too stubborn; they refuse to speak the words I put in their mouths. I'm tired of trying to make something decent out of them," he said as if complaining of his own children. "I keep tearing parts of my soul to patch up theirs; they are wearing me down." The deeper he plunged into his thoughts, the thicker the smoke from his cigarette seemed to become. If melancholy, worry, and odor assumed physical shape, it would turn into a cube the size of his room. I made an effort to push the gloomy thoughts aside, and, as if sensing it, he pleaded, "Ainalaayn, please stay with me."

In the morning, the sun, peering out from behind the mountain crags, forced Almaty to jump out of bed earlier than usual—like a boiling, bubbling cauldron, its streets had already been full of noise and commotion. But the hollow mouths of the ever-multiplying empty bottles on his desk stretched their necks out as if saying, "Drink some more." Unsure if I was disgusted by his drunken state or his shabby appearance, I said arrogantly, "Next time, please don't bother me by calling me here merely to entertain yourself."

"What if the only accessible thing that gives me happiness and peace is you?"

"So you think I'm accessible? You're mistaken; I'm out of your reach!"

"How much are you worth?"

"Right now, your pocket is not deep enough to afford me!"

I didn't remember if we said goodbye to each other.

The news of his death felt like a sharp gulp of air on a gut-wrenchingly freezing November night. I recalled our last meeting that must have left him thinking of me as a greedy, wily woman, and a feeling of shame burned my insides. My grief deepened when I realized I couldn't tell anyone about losing my soulmate.

The tears of his wife crying unconsolably by his coffin was such a lovely sight. How lucky was she to have people say kind words to her, I thought, unable to take my eyes off her. I couldn't even cry then. Why do I bother searching for characters? What if I write about this person who is on my mind now? Right away, I begin recalling the details and writing them down. I put the sentences together. I paint portraits with words.

"He would swallow before speaking. Perhaps, he wanted to weigh some of the coarser words that came to his mind and slightly soften them before uttering them…"

2019

Cover art: Möldir Qarubaiqyzy

Cover design: Amandine Forest

Typesetting and E-book production: Abbas Jaffary

Editor: Deborah Smith

Proofreader: Mayada Ibrahim

Acquiring Editors: Deborah Smith and Saba Ahmed

Publishing Assistant: Nguyễn Đỗ Phương Anh

Marketing Manager: Trà My Hickin

Managing Editor: Mayada Ibrahim

Rights Director: Julia Sanches

Publisher: Kristen Vida Alfaro

Made with Hederis

Printed and bound by Clays Ltd, Elcograf S.p.A.

ABOUT TILTED AXIS PRESS

Tilted Axis publishes mainly work by Asian and African writers, translated into a variety of Englishes. This is an artistic project, for the benefit of readers who would not otherwise have access to the work – including ourselves. We publish what we find personally compelling.

Founded in 2015, we are based in the UK, a state whose former and current imperialism severely impacts writers in the majority world. This position, and those of our individual members, informs our practice, which is also an ongoing exploration into alternatives – to the hierarchisation of certain languages and forms, including forms of translation; to the monoculture of globalisation; to cultural, narrative, and visual stereotypes; to the commercialisation and celebrification of literature and literary translation.

We value the work of translation and translators through fair, transparent pay, public acknowledgement, and respectful communication. We are dedicated to improving access to the industry, through translator mentorships, paid publishing internships, open calls and guest curation.

Our publishing is a work in progress – we are always open to feedback, including constructive criticism, and suggestions for collaborations. We are particularly keen to connect with Black and indigenous translators of Asian and African languages.

tiltedaxispress.com
@TiltedAxisPress